HIS UNEXPECTED BABY BOMBSHELL

HIS UNEXPECTED BABY BOMBSHELL

BY

SORAYA LANE

First published in Great Britain 2015
by Mills & Boon, an imprint of Harlequin (UK) Limited,
Large Print edition 2015
Eton House, 18-24 Paradise Road,
Richmond, Surrey, TW9 1SR

ISBN: 978-0-263-25688-8

Harlequin (UK) Limited's policy is to use papers that are natural, renewable and recyclable products and made from wood grown in sustainable forests. The logging and manufacturing processes conform to the legal environmental regulations of the country of origin.

Printed and bound in Great Britain
by CPI Antony Rowe, Chippenham, Wiltshire

For Carly and Kathryn. I truly feel like
I hit the editor jackpot with the two of you!
Thank you for all your wonderful ideas, and
for making my books so much stronger.

CHAPTER ONE

REBECCA STEWART GULPED as the door to the restaurant opened. *Ben McFarlane.* It had been almost four years, but she'd have known him anywhere. Dark blond hair cropped short, broad shoulders stretching the material of his T-shirt and a stare that still managed to make her heart beat too fast. He was exactly as she remembered him and then some.

"Long time no see."

His gaze softened as he came closer, the corners of his mouth turning upward into a smile, but she could tell he was angry. Those eyes had caused her heart to break and heal all over again so many years ago, the last night they'd had together still burned into her memory as if it was yesterday. *She knew every expression he had.*

Rebecca swallowed, smiled back, her stomach

flip-flopping. *He didn't know. Couldn't* know. That angry gaze, determined stride...she'd thought he was coming in with a purpose when she'd first recognized him. That he knew about his daughter.

She pushed those thoughts away and tried to remind herself of how they'd been before that night, back when they'd been best friends and nothing more.

"Hey, stranger," she said. "I had no idea you were back."

Rebecca moved out from around the counter, hands smoothing the soft cotton of her apron. She didn't know what to do—whether to embrace him, touch him. What did you do to a man, formerly your best friend, once your lover, who you hadn't seen or heard from in years?

"Hey." His voice was surprisingly gruff.

Rebecca stepped into his arms when he opened them, gingerly at first, until he pulled her in, giving her an awkward kind of bear hug. She tried to relax, focusing on breathing in and out. *They were just friends*. But after all this time he still had that effect on her. The smell of his cologne, the strength of his body, everything about him took her back to that night, when a decade of friendship had turned into something more. The night before he'd left and she'd encouraged him to leave her behind even though it had shattered her heart into a million pieces.

"How are you, Bec? Haven't heard from you in a while."

Ouch. The hug must have been a formality.

She took a step back, his hands falling from her waist. It was warm but she shivered, wrapping one arm about her body, the other hanging awkwardly at her side.

"I've been good, Ben. Really good," she said, forcing a big smile, avoiding the question. It wasn't as if he'd emailed her lately, either.

"Your folks?"

Rebecca smiled. Her parents would love to know that Ben was back in town.

"They're great." This time she didn't have to force the grin. "Very busy, enjoying their retirement, so I'm running this place on my own most of the time."

She looked over her shoulder, catching a glimpse of commotion in the kitchen. When she turned back to Ben she noticed he was watching, taking everything in. He'd known her parents' Italian restaurant just as well as she had when they were teenagers. They'd both worked waiting tables over their last summer break, before he'd had the opportunity of a lifetime and left for Argentina.

"Anyway, how about you? What brings you back?"

Ben jammed both hands into his jeans pockets, eyes down before he looked up and met her stare. She knew something was wrong. Why was he even back here?

"Has something happened to your grandfather?" Rebecca heard the falter in her own voice.

"He's not doing great, even though he'd hate me telling you that." He squared his shoulders and pushed his feet out wider. "It was time to come home anyway. I've done my time overseas, for now."

"Really? It's not like you were getting too old to play." She ran her eyes over his superfit frame. He was all muscle, *all athlete*. It wasn't like polo players had a use-by date, so long as they were still performing, and she'd never expected him to give up his career voluntarily. Not for anything.

That made him laugh. "I'm not too old, and I'm fit as hell, so don't go feeling sorry for me." His voice was dry. "I just decided I'd been away for long enough, and Gus needs the help. Argentina was fun, but I missed the old fella."

Oh. She tried to digest his words. It sent a cold streak down her spine. "So you're back for good?"

"Yeah, for the time being, anyway," he said. "If you'd been better at emailing me back, I might have given you a heads-up."

Ouch again. "Ben, I just got busy and there was so much happening. I'm sorry." She knew it sounded like a cop-out, and it was. But he hadn't emailed for a long time, so it wasn't all her fault.

He looked up, gave her a long, hard stare before training his eyes past her head.

"So tell me, how long have you been back? What are your plans?" she asked.

"I'm just playing it by ear. I'll see how it goes, how much I can do around the farm."

Rebecca tried not to react, digested the information as if it meant nothing to her. Polo had always been his life, his dream to play as a career, and now he'd just given it up like that? As if it wasn't the single most important thing to him after years of being desperate to make it happen?

"So that's it. You're just not going to play anymore?" she asked.

A shrug of his shoulders told her he was uncertain. Ben always pushed them up, then hunched them when he was uncomfortable.

"Things change, Bec. You know how it is."

Yeah, she did. Only she was pretty certain that he hadn't just had a change of heart—something else had to be going on. If he was doing it for Gus, she completely understood, but she smelled a rat.

"Anyway, I've only just arrived back in. I'm still going to be training horses, I'm just taking time out from playing." He smiled. "I'm heading for Geelong in the morning."

Rebecca turned and walked back toward the counter, trying to ignore the rising heat in her cheeks. Her pulse had started hammering hard at her temple. *Geelong.* The place where his grandfather's horse training establishment was. The place she'd spent every school vacation and weekend, hanging out with Ben and dreaming about their future. Only she hadn't realized how much of a man's sport polo was—she'd ended up bravely waving Ben off while she stayed behind. It had been tough for him to make it, and even tougher for her to try to make a career out of it. But they'd only been friends, it wasn't as if he'd left his girlfriend behind.

"My granddad turned eighty last week, and I know the cancer's probably worse than he's letting on. I'm heading there to learn everything I can and slowly take the reins from him. Excuse the pun."

"He must be so happy to have you back," Rebecca said, refusing to think about what-ifs just because Ben was back in town and standing before her. It wouldn't have mattered if he'd stayed or not, they'd both wanted different things, and their one night together had been the result of too much to drink. He hadn't owed her anything. She took a deep breath. "You're going to love being home."

He smiled, but his eyes told a different story. He was annoyed with her, and she didn't know what to say to him except sorry for not staying in touch. But she hadn't been able to keep emailing him and not mention what was going on in her life, which meant that losing contact with him had been the only option. She'd always sworn that if he came back she'd tell him, but the guys he played polo with had become his family, he'd always said he loved what he did and wouldn't give it up for anything.

"It was what we always talked about, huh? The two of us playing polo overseas then coming back to run a horse stud together."

"Yeah," she said softly, not wanting to go back in time because thinking about the past only hurt. "Yeah, it was."

"But, anyway, tell me about you? I heard a terrible rumor yesterday that you have a daughter." He chuckled. "Is it true?"

Rebecca placed one hand on the stainless steel counter, trying to stop the quiver as it ran up and down her body. *Her daughter.* How much did he know? *She'd wanted to be the one to tell him.*

"Yeah, I'm a mom now," she said, struggling to keep her voice steady and her breathing even. "To Lexie."

"Lexie," he repeated the name, the word on his lips sending another wave of worry down her back. "And who's the lucky man?"

"Man?" she asked.

"Your husband?"

Gulp. Husband. *Hmm.* "I, ah, well, there is no lucky someone. It's just me and Lexie."

"You mean some bastard left you, after you'd had his child? That why you didn't stay in touch with me? Because you knew I'd hunt him down?"

She did *not* like where this was going. Mmm, what did she say. *Yes, Ben, and that bastard was you? That's exactly why I stopped returning your emails.* But she didn't think of him like that, because she'd made the decision to keep Lexie a secret, to protect both of them, but mainly to make sure she wasn't the one responsible for clipping his wings.

"Let's just say I was better off bringing her up on my own, at least for the time being," Rebecca said, being careful with her words. "My folks have been great and she's a happy little girl, so it's all worked out okay."

The look on Ben's face told her he was unconvinced. "And your dad didn't try to do something about it? Or your brother, for that matter?"

Rebecca needed to change the subject. Fast. She needed time to think about how she was going to tell Ben, how she was going to break it to him. "They weren't thrilled about the whole thing, but sometimes life throws a curve ball and you just have to deal with it."

He opened his mouth, looked grumpy as hell

and about to say something else about her solo parenting situation so she quickly interrupted him.

"Do you want something to eat?" she asked. "We can still rustle up your favorite seafood linguine if you like?"

The frown on Ben's face almost instantly spun upward into a smile. "You still do it?"

"We still *can* do it," she said with a laugh. "It's an oldie but a goodie, that one. Not officially on the lunch menu, but a version of it's still a dinner favorite so we have the ingredients."

This time when he looked at her he didn't break the stare, not for a second. His eyes were locked on hers, his dark brown irises flecked with gold in the bright light.

"I have to go, but how about I take you up on that offer another day? Maybe when you're not so busy and you can join me?"

She forced herself to keep breathing, which felt like the most unnatural thing in the world all of a sudden with Ben standing in front of her. The last thing she needed was to sit down and have lunch with him.

"Sounds good. It would be nice to catch up."

Someone in the kitchen called out her name, giving her an excuse to break away, to finally glance away from the eyes that had been holding her captive.

"I'll see you around, Bec." Ben held his hand up in the air and took a few steps backward before turning and heading for the door.

Rebecca watched him, didn't move a muscle until he'd disappeared from sight, ignoring the chaos behind her. Her heart was thumping with what she knew was excitement, but the rest of her was a quivering mess of nerves, ready to slip into a puddle on the floor. Because there was no part of Ben being back that was okay, none at all.

Ben stuffed his hands deep into his pockets and walked down the street, through the crowded lunchtime buzz of inner city Melbourne. He loved Australia, loved being back on home turf and knowing he was where he belonged. Living overseas had been a blast, but the idea of dividing his time between the city and his granddad's farm was what he wanted now, and he knew he'd made the right decision coming home. As hard as it was leaving his polo family behind, he couldn't stay away from Gus any longer.

And seeing Bec? *Wow.* He'd only been home one day and it had been a fight not to turn up at the restaurant that first night, just to lay eyes on her again. The girl who'd waved him goodbye, his best friend, and then slowly disappeared from his life. But who could blame her? He hadn't exactly been the best at staying in touch, but then she'd been downright terrible.

And then she'd met some other guy and had a kid? Little Bec all grown up and a *mom*? Now, that he hadn't been expecting. In his mind he'd imagined her life on hold, expected he could come home and somehow he'd be able to convince her that their night together had been a good thing, that they were supposed to be more than just friends. He'd been a fool, naive at best, and after seeing her today he knew he'd waited too long, that she'd moved on and he'd missed his chance.

Because even though he'd had the time of his life away, ridden some of the best polo ponies in the world and traveled to the most incredible countries, he'd never stopped thinking about Rebecca. Not for a moment. At the time, he'd been so desperate to belong, loved being part of a big extended polo family, when in reality he'd had a little family here with Gus and Rebecca all along, only it had taken being away so long for him to realize it. It wasn't until his granddad had finally admitted how sick he was that it had really hit home.

Rebecca's soft, smiling face, pillowy lips and shining eyes had been the memory he'd clung on to, and almost four years on, he was darn pleased she didn't have a husband. He could never stay angry with her and seeing her today had proved it. He'd gone in all tough guy, wanting to demand why she'd lost touch. *But he hadn't*. And they might have been drunk that night together, but he hadn't forgotten a moment of what had happened between them.

He'd kill the guy who'd left her, on her own and with a child, and he'd bet her parents would be happy to help him find him. Rebecca had been his best friend, and for one night she'd been his lover. Ben grimaced as he jumped behind the wheel of his car. *And that one night had ruined everything between them.*

Rebecca strolled in to the preschool center and locked eyes on her daughter. Lexie was running around the room at high speed, arms spread out as if she was flying, her little lips bouncing off one another to make a noise like a plane. Her heart fluttered and she turned away, not wanting Lexie to see her yet. Her little girl was clingy enough as it was, and she loved seeing her play with the other kids.

"Hey there."

Bec turned to find Julia, one of the teachers, behind her. She was holding out a colorful, smudged sheet of paper.

"Lexie painted this today and insisted I put it somewhere safe for Mommy."

The grin that followed made her smile, and she reached out to take it. "She has quite a talent, don't you think?"

Both women laughed then as Bec held out the painting and squinted, trying to decipher exactly what it was. "A house covered in green slime?" she guessed.

"Day at the beach?"

A little voice interrupted them. "Mommy!"

Bec turned and scooped up her girl, planting a kiss on her shiny blond head. "Hey, sunshine."

"Do you like my painting?"

"Of course!"

"It's me on a horse. A horse, Mommy!"

"Mmm." She tried not to grin as she looked back at her. The teacher had to walk away to keep from laughing. "We were just saying what a lovely horse it is."

"It's a polo horse." She fought to stand on the ground. "Me on a polo pony."

Rebecca's smile fell from her face, until she realized Lexie was still watching her. She forced her panic away. A polo pony? How did she even know about polo ponies?

"Let's go, sweetheart. Grab your bag and say goodbye to Julia."

She watched as her daughter darted away, reached a hand to push back her hair as she stared at the picture. Lexie had never even been around horses, let alone ridden one, but she'd been obsessed about them since she could say the word. *Just like someone else she knew.* As much as she didn't want to admit it, Lexie was more like her dad than she'd let herself believe.

"Mommy?"

She dropped to her knees, taking the bag from her daughter and zipping it up. "Yes, sweetheart."

"Granddad says you used to ride horses. That you used to ride *polo ponies*."

"Did he now?" She would kill him for even talking to Lexie about her riding. That was a part of her life she'd left behind. She'd never even been near a horse since Ben had left, and she'd long since given up any dreams of making a career out of the sport she'd loved since she was fourteen. The last horse she'd had…she didn't even want to think about the accident.

"He said you were real good, too, until you fell off one day. Did it hurt?"

"And when was Granddad telling you all this?" she asked.

"Yesterday."

Lexie skipped off toward the door, waiting for her, her hand outstretched.

"Can *we* go horse riding?" she asked.

"Maybe."

"Why maybe?"

"I don't know anyone who owns a horse." It was a lie, but what else was she going to say?

"Could *we* get a horse, then?" Lexie asked.

"Get in the car."

She closed the door after her and stood on the sidewalk for a few seconds, eyes closed, taking a deep breath to calm her nerves. Once upon a time she would have done anything to spend her life around horses, but that was in the past, and that was exactly how she wanted to keep it. She had to tell Ben, she knew that, but she still didn't want to go back.

CHAPTER TWO

BEN SMILED AT his granddad and walked over to the young colt. The animal's nostrils were flared, body rigid as he approached him.

"Keep your hands down. Don't touch him until he touches you first."

Ben listened to him, and followed his instructions. More and more he was realizing that his grandfather's instincts were always right. He'd argued with the trainers he worked with overseas until he was blue in the face, and he'd been tired of their old-fashioned attitudes. Some trainers liked to force horses into submission, but that wasn't something they did at McFarlane Stables. Just because half the polo trainers out there thought they were crazy for practicing natural horsemanship didn't mean he was going to change their approach. And it was one of the reasons he'd finally had enough of being overseas, one of the reasons he'd finally broken ties with the guys he'd loved working alongside for so long to come home.

"Good. Once he turns his head in, pat him and then move the rope over his neck."

Ben did as he was told. The horse responded to him, moving quietly, but all hell broke loose once the rope was over.

"Keep hold, even if he goes right out to the end."

A damp line of sweat graced his forehead, but he kept hold. This was the only rough part of the exercise and he hated it, but if he got it right this time, it wouldn't need to be done again. Because *animals* and *force* were not two words he liked used in the same sentence.

The horse stopped bucking and rearing and came to a halt, eyeing him cautiously from a small distance.

"Good boy." He said the words softly before approaching him again. "What a good fella."

"Give him a pat and then put the halter on him," his granddad called out.

Ben moved forward, smiling at the horse as he stood calmly. He gave him a scratch behind the ear and then lifted the halter, rubbing his sweet spots as he did so.

Nice and gentle, Ben reminded himself, reaching up and folding the leather strap over the horse's nose and behind his pricked ears. The horse stood still, ears flickering as he listened to him, accepting what was happening.

Ben stood back and grinned. Working with his grandfather for just one morning was worth having come home for.

"Good job, son. Well done."

He gave the horse one final pat and then opened up the gate out of the yard, letting him canter off over to the other young stock. Ben moved toward his granddad, pleased to see the smile on his weathered face.

"It's in your blood, always has been, always will be."

His granddad's voice was strong and deep, but

the slap he gave Ben on his shoulder wasn't as powerful as it used to be; his gnarled, weathered hands failing him after years of hard work. Gus McFarlane was a strong man, the kind of man who was used to commanding attention when he wanted it, but he was deteriorating fast. There was something the old man wasn't telling him, he just knew it.

"So have you been coping okay? On your own I mean?"

Gus used a cane, walking slowly over the grass. Mind as sharp as a tack, but the body just not keeping up. Guilt washed over Ben—he'd been so desperate to leave Australia and follow his own dreams, but now that he was back he was seriously regretting leaving his granddad for so long.

"You ever hear from the Stewart girl?"

Ben's body went rigid. "Rebecca? Yeah, well, sort of. I mean, I went to see her when I got back." He tried to sound nonchalant. "Yesterday, actually."

"Great girl that one. You should have married her, you know that, right?"

Yeah, he knew. But Bec was…well, *Bec*. It was never that he hadn't been attracted to her, or that he hadn't wanted her, but he'd always known he could never give her enough and he still couldn't. Settling down with a nice girl just hadn't been part of his plan, what he'd imagined for himself, because he'd always been focused on what he wanted. And now that he didn't have polo, he was at more of a loss about what he wanted from life than he'd ever been.

"She gave up returning my emails a long time ago, Granddad." He wasn't going to let Rebecca off the hook, not when he was getting *the look* from the old man. The fact their friendship had fallen by the wayside was as much her fault as it was his. "And we were only friends, you know that. Nothing more." His granddad didn't need to know they'd spent a night together, and that's all it had been—one night, not a relationship.

"Great little rider, that one. Hard worker and

a good seat in the saddle. Not to mention darn nice to look at."

"Yup," Ben agreed.

"Bring her out here sometime. I've a filly that needs to be ridden by a woman, and there ain't none of them out here anymore."

Ben thought about Bec, about having her out here again. Would she even come if he asked her to? Four years hadn't quelled his desire for her, but things had changed, heck, *she'd* changed.

"She won't have ridden in a long time." He doubted she'd make the trip. "And I'm not sure we're on the best terms." It had been awkward between them the other day, even if he had enjoyed seeing her again.

Gus stopped then, resting heavily on his cane. "Don't matter how long it's been, because a woman like her? She's a natural, just like you." He chuckled. "And unless she's already married, don't be a quitter, son. You don't give up on her if she's what you want."

Ben cleared his throat. His grandfather was unbelievable—he'd only been home a few days and already he was giving him advice on his love life.

"I haven't got long now, doc said maybe only six months. I'm not gonna beat the cancer this time, son." He shrugged. "Tell Rebecca I want to see her. What kind of girl would say no to a dying old man, huh?"

It was his turn to give Gus a slap on the shoulder. Thinking about his granddad dying was not something Ben wanted to give in to, and if the old man wanted Rebecca, then who was he to say no?

"We'll be right, Granddad. Cancer won't beat you."

But it would and they both knew it.

"Table six! No menus yet."

Rebecca hurried to the kitchen as the bell dinged. She hated keeping her customers waiting, especially the regulars she saw seated at her tables every week.

"Phone for you, Bec."

"Take a message," she hollered back.

"Sure?"

She gave the young waiter a hard stare and he shrugged. Who the hell would be calling her during a lunch shift?

She placed the empty plates down and hurried out back.

"It wasn't about Lexie was it?" She regretted her sharp tone and gave the young guy a smile.

"Nah, someone called Ben. Said you'd know how to get in touch."

The name hit her like a thump to her lungs. *Ben.* Why was he calling here? She glanced around, saw that everything was under control and stepped back from the counter. "I'm taking ten," she called out, heading out the back door, suddenly desperately in need of fresh air and sunlight.

She ignored the noise of the city, the streets filled with all kinds of people rushing back and forward, and took a deep breath, pulling her mobile from her pocket. She should have ignored his call, stopped thinking about what she'd had with Ben before he left, but it was an impossible task and she knew it.

Seeing Ben had reminded her, what they were both missing out on, of how nice it would be to have a man around. *Not just any man, but a Ben kind of man.* But she'd made the decision to let him go without saying anything about how she felt, and no amount of regrets was going to change that.

And now she had to decide whether to return his call or not. *And at the same time figure out what the hell I'm going to do about telling him he has a daughter.*

She bit down hard on her lower lip and dialed the number, quickly as if the speed was going to make a difference. The number was still ingrained in her memory, digits that she had never, ever forgotten. Hell, it had once been her favorite number, and not just for Ben being at the other end of it. Because Gus had been as much her lifeline back then as Ben had. When he'd offer her a ride it had been like a junkie getting a fix.

She kept repeating the number in her mind, silently, lips barely moving as it rung.

"McFarlane Stables."

Phew. It wasn't Ben.

"Gus!" At least she didn't have to hide her excitement with him. "I've missed you so much."

"I don't have many young ladies call me, so I'm guessing that's you, Rebecca."

His voice was strong, but it crackled more than it used to. Those soft, kind tones that had soothed her and taught her when she was a girl—he'd been the grandfather she'd always wished was her own.

"How did you guess?"

His laughter rumbled down the line. "Something to do with me telling that grandson of mine to get you out here before I kick the bucket."

"Gus! Don't talk like that."

"Ah, but it's true, love."

"*Gus,*" she said, not knowing what else to say to the man she still cared so much about.

"Let's not talk morbid. Just promise me you're coming to see us."

The silence was all her doing this time. She hadn't expected an invitation to McFarlane's, in fact, she hadn't even considered the possibility of going back there. But it was tempting, just the thought of taking a step back in the past even if it was just for a few hours.

"So, are you coming or not?" He never had been one to waste words.

"I, ah..." She'd kept her secret for so long, the last thing she needed was for it to all unravel now before she had time to figure everything out and deal with it properly, and she'd have to ask her folks to look after Lexie.

"Rebecca?"

A tightness in her throat made it hard for her to say *anything.* "Well..." She paused. "Yes."

"Yes?"

"How about I come down this Saturday?" she asked.

"Bring your bag, love. I want you to enjoy the weekend here. Got a horse that needs your help."

She choked. The thought of going back in time, of horses, of Gus...*it was hard.* Exciting, thrilling, terrifying...but still hard.

"I'll tell the boy you're coming."

Uh-oh. The silver-tongued old fox had talked

her into a weekend away, all without a hint of protest from her, and she'd forgotten about the reality of Ben. About the fact that it wasn't just going to be her and Gus reminiscing, that it wasn't about being old friends and catching up. *Just like old times.* That's what he'd said, but there was no way anything between her and Ben was like it used to be.

At least she had nothing to feel guilty about where Lexie was concerned—she spent every Saturday night with her grandparents anyway, but still…she usually didn't feel bad about having Saturday night off from parenting each week because she worked, but having an evening to herself seemed wrong somehow. Even though she'd never done it once in her daughter's three years before.

But she deserved one weekend to herself, and she just couldn't risk taking her with her.

A butterfly-soft shiver ran the length of her spine. But this was Ben, this was a step back into the past for one night, and the idea of seeing him again… She shook her head as if it would somehow push her worries away.

She was going to do it. And then she'd figure out how to break the news to him, because now he was home, and if he was home for good, then all the reasons she had for keeping Lexie from him were gone.

CHAPTER THREE

THIS WAS HARDER than she'd thought. Just the idea of seeing Ben had her stomach turning, twisting into a cavalcade of knots. She focused on the road and gripped the wheel tighter, pulling over just near the turnoff and trying to slow her breathing, trying to stop her hands from trembling, too. If she could only still them enough to smudge some gloss over her dry lips, run her fingers through her hair and press a smidge of perfume to her neck, she'd be fine.

The driveway loomed ahead; as immaculate as she'd remembered it. Gus was an old man now, but his standards hadn't slipped, and she found herself hoping the stables and house were unchanged, too. Her memories were so vivid, colorful in her mind as if she'd been here merely months ago, instead of years.

She pushed the lever down into Drive again, satisfied that she looked passable in the mirror, and pulled slowly into the driveway. Gravel crunched under the tires and trees softly waved against the metal of the vehicle as if welcoming her. Bec took a deep breath and found emotions getting the better of her. Up until a week ago, she'd never expected to see this place again, but it was so good to be back.

Up ahead she could just see the house, a triple brick, beautiful residence that was as immaculate as the drive. Roses were neatly clipped, windows thrown wide, one of the most gorgeous houses she'd ever seen. Her own family home was nice, better than modest, but this place was something else. And then her eyes settled on her once favorite part of the property—the row of stables, in an L-shape, to the left of the house.

She slowed the car to a crawl as she surveyed the place, looking for any sign of life and seeing none. There were no horses in sight, but then at this time of day it wasn't to be expected. Apart from a ginger cat stretched out in the sun, it was as good as deserted. In a way she was glad, it gave her time to walk around and reminisce before figuring out what to say to Ben.

She pushed open the car door and let it shut behind her as she stretched her legs. The sun was warm on her bare arms and she moved toward the stables, eyes wandering everywhere. What she loved about this place was the privacy, with only the side of the stables visible. Bec had heard there were fewer horses here than ever now that Gus had slowed down, but as soon as she rounded the building it became obvious that reduced numbers for him were still impressive.

The property had been purpose built with horse rearing and polo playing in mind. The old stables had been meticulously cared for and maintained over the years, and Rebecca stopped to look. The stables stretched in a long line, flanked by larger, box stalls tying up bays. The wooden structures were faded yet clean, the white and navy colors still vivid in her mind from years ago. Wisteria curled down over the edges, pots of bright flowers infusing color into the well-kept area. The door to the tack room was wide-open, and Rebecca could smell the aroma of saddle soap and sweaty horse blankets. It was a blast from the past that made her smile.

She continued on, stopping to rub a nose poking out from one of the boxes. The smell of hay, the sight of horseflesh, it sent a shiver of both excitement and worry through her body. The same kind of feeling she got thinking about Ben.

Rebecca looked ahead to the land before her. The most sheltered field was still kept for young stock, and from the looks of them, recently weaned fillies and colts. Frisky-looking babies who were having a ball of a time, playing and scolding one another in the safe, well-fenced environment. Working with the young stock had been something she and Ben had both enjoyed. Teaching them their manners, how to respect humans, all without needing to use a firm hand. Back then, she and Ben had always had their heads buried in a Monty Roberts book, the legendary horse whisperer who flaunted industry-standard horse breaking rules.

Rebecca walked on and let her eyes wander, taking in the sights, but it was the noise out to her right that had the blood pumping that little bit faster in her veins, that had a smile turning her mouth upward.

She could just make out someone, who she presumed was Gus, excitedly waving what looked to be a cane as some young guys trained. At least six horses rushed past in a blur, hooves pounding hard on the ground as they thundered fast alongside each other. Her feet picked up speed and she rushed toward them, desperately wanting to watch the game as the horses and riders galloped around the polo field.

She didn't want to disturb Gus, so she approached quietly once she was close, watching the riders compete for the ball, heading toward the goal. From her vantage point, she snuck a quick glance at the old man before her and felt sad, it was like he'd shrunk a little and aged so quickly, but it was unmistakably the same kind person who had been so good to her for so many years.

"Go, go, go!" She jumped as Gus screamed, waving his stick again.

As one of the players made a goal he threw his stick, one hand pumping up in a fist. She couldn't help but laugh.

"Gus." Her voice was soft but he turned immediately on the spot, his eyes meeting hers.

Gus looked her over for a moment before a big smile spread out wide over his face.

"Rebecca! Well, look at you."

He held out his arms and she reached him in no time, embracing him fondly.

"It's so good to be back here, to see you," she mumbled, holding him tight.

He smiled at her as she stepped back, his eyes shining.

"Just look at you. Look at you, huh? All grown-up."

She beamed, embarrassed yet flattered. Before she could answer a voice interrupted them, sending her almost a foot in the air with fright.

"Becca."

Ben. She would recognize that voice anywhere.

Deep, rich and delicious. He sat astride a blowing, sweaty polo pony that was now dancing very close to her.

"Good goal, son. I'll walk him back for you."

Ben jumped to the ground and passed Gus the reins.

"You sure you're okay taking him?"

The older man just looked skyward, eyes rolling. Bec knew it would take more than a highly strung horse to keep him from where the action was, walking cane or not.

Bec stole a glance at Ben while his attention was still directed at the horse before looking away. If only he wasn't so handsome, so charming, so…*not available*. Or possibly available, she had no idea if he had a girlfriend or not, but not available to her. She was all about no complications, being a mother, nothing else. *Nothing else*, she repeated inside her head just in case her body was thinking of disagreeing. She'd been happy being friends with him for so long, but ever since that night…

"Hey."

He was talking to her. *Damn it!* And there she was away in fairyland.

"You looked good out there." It was all she could think to say, but the truth was she hadn't even realized he was the one in the saddle.

"Yeah, well, I'm happy to be home, but I'm still craving some saddle time." He grinned at her and pulled his helmet off, turning toward the field where some of the guys were still training, and ran a hand through his short hair. "You ever think about getting back up again?"

It had been a long time for her, a dream she'd long since given up, and now she was a mom she was way more cautious than she'd once been. The allure of the polo field now was more about watching than actually doing. And besides, that fall had almost broken her. It had taken everything away from her; her dreams, her future. And Ben.

"Maybe," she lied. Or maybe it wasn't a lie. Being back here was giving her all sorts of mixed emotions, making her question everything. "It's not something I've really thought about, to be honest."

Ben turned to her then and reached out a hand, touching her arm so lightly she almost wondered if she was imagining it.

"It's great to have you here, Bec."

She struggled for words, her skin tingling where he'd touched her. They'd been best friends for years, before one night had changed everything, and now she could hardly look at him without thinking about the fact she'd seen him naked. *And how darn good he'd looked.*

"It feels good being back here." She hardly trusted her voice.

He started to walk and she followed his lead, his long legs eating up the ground.

"There's something about this place, Bec. It's good for the soul."

He stopped then, turning to face her, pulling her hands into his and holding them tight. He studied her with such intensity she didn't know where to look or what to say.

"I'm sorry, Bec, for expecting you to stay in

touch after what happened, for leaving you in the first place," he said, his voice low. "I never stopped thinking about you, but it all just got so complicated. So much for best friends, huh?"

Until we ruined it. They were the unspoken words hanging between them.

Bec gulped, her eyes burning with tears. Their friendship? Was that all he wanted from her? Lexie's beautiful little face flashed before her and she almost told him, so wanted to tell him that he was the father of her beautiful daughter, but she didn't. Couldn't yet, even though she knew she had to. Because she also knew that he never wanted children—he'd told her since they were in high school that he wasn't ever going to be a dad after what he'd been through—and she knew nothing would ever change his mind. But she couldn't deny him the chance, couldn't keep this from him any longer.

"I've missed you, Ben. But things change, and I guess we just grew apart, right?"

"Maybe we should have both stuck to our plan. Gone to the UK together and both played."

"It would have been good, huh?" Only the reality was that Ben had been picked up by a team in Argentina, and she hadn't, and instead of telling him the truth, she'd made out like she couldn't leave her family. That it wasn't what she wanted. Maybe if he'd asked her to go as more than friends, maybe if her confidence hadn't been shattered after the fall and she'd not been such a mess over everything. Maybe then things could or would have been different.

His eyes were as sad as hers as he watched her. "Come on, let's show you around. There's something I want you to see."

Her eyebrows dragged together as he turned and started to walk again, tugging her along with him.

"Well, more like Gus wants you to see it. Just come and take a look."

Her curiosity was piqued, and she hurried to keep up with him. Make her hair longer, she thought, take away the soft crinkles around his eyes and they could have gone back five or so years. To a time when everything had seemed possible, when they were both in charge of their own destinies, before fate and life had intervened. Before she'd fallen pregnant to a man she'd loved with all her heart, and instead of asking him to stay behind because she loved him, she'd let him go. She couldn't help but wonder if he would have left and not come home, had she told him how she really felt. If she'd called him and told him that she was pregnant. But then deep down she knew the answer to that.

Ben would *never* have left her, not if he knew how she felt, if he knew that she was carrying his baby. And that was precisely why she'd lied, told him they'd made a mistake that night, that they were better as friends. Because she didn't believe in clipping the wings of a bird to keep it at home, and Ben had been like an eagle ready to soar through the sky. And she never wanted to be responsible for ruining Ben's life, and seeing him repeat the same mistakes his mother had.

CHAPTER FOUR

"SHE'S BEAUTIFUL."

Rebecca ran her eyes over every inch of the horse. It wasn't hard to act interested—the filly was one of the most beautiful animals she had ever seen. Endless black legs, four white socks and a silky long tail. Her face was framed by a wide white blaze, stretching all the way to her nostrils; dark brown eyes like pools of trust, following every movement she and Ben made.

He didn't say anything, just watched the horse, arms slung over the corral fence, one foot resting on the lowest tread of timber.

"So, what's the deal with her?"

Ben shrugged, broad shoulders moving under his shirt. She was glad to have the distraction of the horse, because she was finding it almost impossible not to stare at him.

"She's had all the guys on, doesn't seem to like them."

"How about you?" Rebecca asked. "Does she like you?"

He laughed. "Nope, not particularly."

They looked at one another. They were both thinking the same thing, Rebecca could tell by the look in his eyes. There had always been the odd horse that had worked better for one of them or the other, it was about personalities, the rider clicking with beast. But there had been one very special mare who'd only ever worked for Rebecca, to the point where Gus had decided the horse was useless for anyone else, and had given her over to Bec. It had all worked well, her dream come true to own such an amazing mare, until the accident. She'd lost her nerve, and her will to ride, and her beautiful mare had lost her life. The memory flash made her skin prickle. And then she'd lost her best friend, all in the course of a couple of months, as well as her dreams of making it big in the polo world. She'd never gotten over that period in her life, had always just pushed it from her mind, but her pain was still raw.

Ben let out a big breath of air and gave her a smile—a slow rise of his mouth, followed by a gentle wink. It was as if he had put his arm around her, comforted her, just by looking at her. No one else had ever made her feel quite like Ben could. Embraced, comforted, cared for, all in a single look. Pity it had taken her so many years to figure out that she was in love with him. When they'd finally taken that step, he was gone, and then she went from losing a friend to nursing a broken heart. Ben had never said anything, never told her that he thought of her as any more than a friend, and so she'd just kept her mouth shut and let him get on with his life.

"So what do you think?"

Rebecca raised her eyes. *What did she think*? Her mind was racing, took her a moment to remember what they were even talking about. And then she glanced at the filly before them.

Ben was watching her, waiting for her answer. But here, back on a horse again, after all this time?

"I, ah, don't think so."

Ben stepped up onto the railing and hauled himself into the corral. "If I persist long enough, she'll let me catch her, but she's wild when anyone tries to get near her."

"And you expect me to do what you guys can't?"

Ben walked backward until his back was pressed against the wooden rails, before climbing up to sit on the fence.

"You know you can do it, Bec."

Rebecca stayed on the other side of the fence, close to Ben but not quite touching. It was tempting, she could admit that, but there was no way she was up to it. No way she could summon the courage to climb on a spirited horse and stay calm enough and confident enough to be in control. Not after all this time.

"What's her name?"

Ben turned and smiled. "That mean you're ready to give it a go?"

She laughed, shaking her head as she looked back at the horse. No, all it meant was she was trying to change the subject.

"Missy," he told her. "Her name's Missy."

Rebecca kept watching the horse. *Missy.* She played the name through her mind. It was a pretty name, but it didn't make any difference. She wasn't going near her.

"What do you say?"

"Just give me some time." The words came out before she could think longer. And she wasn't even sure she was still talking about horses.

Ben jumped off the fence and landed on the hard packed dirt, his feet falling inches away from hers. Rebecca had a funny feeling she would live to regret that comment. There was no way he was going to let her leave at the end of this weekend without trying her luck with that horse, and the very idea terrified her. She didn't know if it was simply losing her nerve or just the years of not riding catching up on her, but she couldn't even comprehend climbing back into the saddle, with or without Ben egging her on.

He stood close to her, too close, and their eyes met for just a second. It was long enough to feel like one second too long, though. Neither of them knew what to say. Ben because he wasn't the type to just come out and say something, and her because she had too much to hide. Too much at stake. Just being with him was a risk, or at least it was until she was ready to come clean and tell him what she'd done. It wasn't that she was going to keep it from him, she just wanted to do it right, to break it to him the right way, if that was even possible.

Rebecca walked beside Ben. She was listening to him but her eyes were floating around their surroundings, drinking in the familiar sights she had gone so long without seeing.

"What do you think?"

She turned her attention back to Ben. She had no idea what he was talking about. *Again.*

Gus appeared ahead of them and saved her from having to answer. He leaned against the corner of the stable block, resting a leg, but he was smiling. Rebecca guessed that he was probably feeling worse than he let on, but this was his life. The alternative was to cart him off to hospital, or a rest home, and what good would that do him? He deserved to be here till his last day, doing what he loved.

"So when are you two going off for a ride?"

Rebecca laughed and glanced at Ben. She hoped that he hadn't put his grandfather up to it. "I'm not sure I'll be riding at all this weekend. These days I prefer my feet firmly on the ground."

"Do you remember Willy?" Gus asked

She nodded. "Who could forget him?" Although as she said it, she was wondering if it was a trick question. "He must be, what? Twenty…twenty-two years old now?" He'd been Gus's horse when she was a teenager. The most reliable, safe, sweet horse she'd ever come across, and he'd been Gus's pride and joy.

"Sure is. I can't ride anymore and he's going to waste just sitting around. Thought he could do with a walk around the farm. What do you say?"

Rebecca took a step backward and walked straight smack bang into Ben. He must have stopped right behind her, his large frame preventing her from making a getaway. She lurched forward and felt trapped. Backward meant into Ben and forward meant the horse. She didn't know what scared her more. Her heart was hammering, although the idea of falling back into the warmth of Ben's body was sounding like the more attractive option right now.

"I, ah, I don't know, Gus. Really, I…"

"Are you telling me you came all the way here without your riding gear?"

Gulp. He had her there. Yes, she had brought it, but with no intention of actually *putting it on*. She eyed up the horse some more and felt a lump of genuine terror knot in her throat, but at least riding would give her a distraction aside from Ben.

"How about it, Bec?"

Ben placed his hands on either side of her arms, still standing behind her. It was nothing more than a gentle press of his skin against hers, but it sent a butterfly-soft shiver down her back. He was too close and it was only making her feel more guilty about everything, like a traitor for even being there.

Gus was watching her, Ben was touching her, even the horse seemed to be staring at her, waiting for her answer.

"Okay fine, I'll do it."

Maybe it was the pressure, the sun making her giddy, hell, it might have even been the way Ben was looking at her, but she felt her resolve buckle. But all of a sudden going for a trail ride didn't seem like the stupidest idea in the world.

"Okay?" Ben seemed doubtful, and Gus winked before leaving them to it.

"Don't sound so surprised," she muttered.

She knew this was only the start of it, or maybe it wasn't. Because once she told Ben the truth he'd never forgive her, and then she'd never be invited back ever again.

"Do you want to go get changed?" Ben asked.

He looked her up and down, and Rebecca tried not to laugh as a smile kicked the corners of her mouth up. "I've never ridden in a sundress and sandals before, and I'm not about to start."

She turned and headed back to the car as Ben laughed, wanting to look back at him but not letting herself. There was something about Ben, there always had been; a quiet strength about him that she'd been drawn to when they were both only at school, and that confidence had translated into a super sexy guy. There was nothing arrogant about him even though he'd played with the best polo players in the world, and his manner with animals? That had always set him apart from any man she'd ever met before. *And it was why he'd be such a darn good father.* She swallowed hard and tried not to think about what-ifs—Ben had made it clear he wasn't ever going to have a family of his own, that he wouldn't ever repeat the mistakes his own mom had made, and she knew that his hurt ran so deep that nothing, *nothing*, was capable of changing his mind. Which was why she'd kept her secret all this time. But now it was time for him to decide, for him to be the one to make that choice.

She tugged the car door open and grabbed her bag. All of her other belongings were in a small suitcase, but her riding clothes were in the same bag they'd always been in. She pulled back the zip and just looked at them for a moment, before sucking up all her jitters and swallowing them away.

She looked around to check she was alone, then took off her sandals and replaced them with socks and pulled her jodhpurs over her ankles and up her thighs. The material stretched tight, but she was pleased to be able to do the waist up. Years on, not to mention one child later, and she could still fit into the tight breeches—it was a good feeling.

Rebecca tugged her dress over her shoulders and placed it on the backseat, before grabbing her former favorite faded gray Pearl Jam T-shirt she had once worn on a daily basis. She searched for a tie in the glove box and then yanked her hair into a plait, before grabbing her helmet and gloves and closing the car door.

This was it. It was now or never.

Ben emerged from around the side of the stables, sitting astride a striking chestnut horse, and leading Willy on his left. She drew in a big breath of air and marched onward, trying hard to keep her smile from faltering.

"You look good."

His words made her smile, even if she didn't believe him for a second. "Liar liar pants on fire," she joked. "But thanks for the compliment."

"Need a hand getting on?" he asked.

"Nah, I'm fine." She was lying, but she'd rather struggle on without any assistance from Ben. His hands anywhere near her body right now was not a good idea.

She took the reins and lifted her left leg, hopping on one foot as she tried to get it high enough to get her left one through the stirrup.

"Not quite as flexible as you used to be, huh?"

Ben dismounted and moved to help her. Heat flooded Rebecca's face as he touched her shoulder, laughing softly.

"If it makes you feel any better, some of the guys I rode with in Argentina spent half their lives on horseback and could only mount if they were standing on a fence."

Rebecca grimaced. She hadn't realized that getting *on* the horse would be the tough part.

"Here."

Ben cupped his hands and indicated for her to put her knee up. She did, his strong palms closing around her leg, sending spasms of warmth through her body.

"Thanks," she said. "On three."

She bounced three times before Ben sprang her into the air, and straight on to Willy's back. She landed with a soft thump and felt that all too familiar turmoil in her stomach. The accident hit her memory bank like it was yesterday.

She was about to jump straight off when Ben placed a hand to her thigh, almost sending her flying off the other side. All those years they had touched, slept side by side in sleeping bags, sat close, and there had never been a reaction like that. It was as if that one night all those years ago was still pulling them together; their skin still reactive to the pressure of one another's touch. His hand felt hot, heating through the fabric of her jodhpurs, and she knew he felt it, too.

"You're okay," he soothed, never taking his eyes off her.

She swallowed a lump that felt as big as a rock and nodded. Suddenly the horse seemed like the safe bet.

Ben raised his other hand to shield his eyes from the sun, gave her one of his sexy-as-heck winks and then turned back to his horse.

"You'll be just fine."

All of a sudden she knew she was right. It wasn't the horse she needed to be scared of. Danger had just looked her straight in the eye and she'd managed to survive it. For now.

CHAPTER FIVE

REBECCA FINALLY STARTED to relax. Her back had been rigid, legs clammy and neck stiff. She wondered if she'd even been breathing for fear of falling off.

"I guess this is why they say to get straight back in the saddle after a fall."

Ben was riding slightly ahead of her but he reined back to match her horse's stride.

"Sometimes that's easier said than done," he said.

"I've kept something from you all this time, Ben," she admitted. It was almost impossible preparing to confess this, let alone telling him her big secret. *Baby steps*, she just needed to take baby steps.

He turned to watch her, eyebrows raised in question.

Rebecca sighed, looking away from him. She'd told him at the time that she'd turned down the offer she'd been made, that she'd decided she just didn't want to leave her family and live overseas anymore. "I lied to you," she said simply. "I was never offered a position on the women's team, but I didn't want to hold you back, and then after my fall, I didn't even know if I wanted to play anymore."

When he never replied, the only sound their horses' hooves echoing on the dirt, she braved a glance at him. From side on his jaw looked like it was cut from steel, his entire face like stone.

"You shouldn't have done that." His voice was deep and gravelly. "I wouldn't have just left you like that if I'd…"

"And that's why I did it. I wasn't going to make you second-guess what you wanted. We were only friends, right?" Just saying it hurt her. "It wasn't like you were walking out on your girlfriend."

"So you lied and told me you couldn't leave your family? That staying behind was what you wanted? That we just didn't share the same dreams anymore?" He grunted. "And we might not have been dating, Bec, but we were damn good friends. We'd always planned on going together."

She knew he was angry, but she'd needed to tell him.

"I just wanted you to know the truth, Ben. It was a long time ago, but still."

He made a grunting noise again, his shoulders bunched. "You still shouldn't have lied to me."

"I was a mess after everything that happened," she said. "I was still dreaming of making a team when in reality I was terrified at the idea of even getting on a horse and playing a game again. And then you…" She let her voice trail off, not really wanting to open up to him about how she'd felt. "I lost everything. My confidence was shattered and I was a mess."

"I would have tried to help you, Bec. I wouldn't have just walked away if I'd known the truth."

And that's why she hadn't told him. She hadn't wanted to clip his wings, would never have done that to him, but there had also been a little voice in her head telling her that after everything that had happened, she hadn't been good enough for him anymore. That he wouldn't want her if she couldn't even muster the courage to get back in the saddle and try to make another team.

They rode in silence, Rebecca staring straight ahead, her nerves about being on horseback slowly disappearing. It was a strange feeling being nervous about a sport that had once been her life.

"So how do you feel right now?" Ben asked.

Bec relaxed her grip on the reins and sat deep in the saddle, actually loving how good it felt. The start of a smile was tugging at the corners of her mouth and she couldn't resist the pull. Maybe he was going to let bygones be bygones, which meant that she had to do the same.

"You know what?" She grinned over at him, trying to push the past out of her mind, at least for the afternoon. "Now that I'm not hanging on for dear life, it feels kinda good."

"How about a canter down to the creek?"

Ben was sitting straight-backed, comfortable in the saddle, his broad shoulders stretched wide. There was something about seeing him in his white T-shirt, jeans and baseball cap that sent her back years in her mind. He probably felt the same looking at her.

She sucked up her courage and shortened her reins. "Just remember that I'm not the rider I used to be."

She clucked Willy first into a trot and then into his rocking horse canter. Rebecca moved back and forth, feeling her legs stretch out, calf muscles groaning with the movement. There was nothing particularly easy about riding all over again, but it was a bit like the old bike theory. Once you knew how, it was something you never truly forgot.

"Doing good, *cowgirl*, doing good," called Ben with a cowboy drawl.

Rebecca stayed focused, still expecting Willy

to do something out of the ordinary, but he behaved like a complete gentleman.

Ben pulled back to a walk and Rebecca followed his lead, her chest rising rapidly with the burst of exercise.

"It's just up there." He pointed.

"Uh-huh." Her lungs were screaming for more air—she wasn't capable of saying anything else.

They rode in silence the rest of the way, and Rebecca felt those darn butterflies ignite in her stomach again. Ben was gorgeous and charming and so easy to be around, and he hadn't even given her that much of a grilling over the whole lie. He deserved to know about Lexie, too, once she figured out how to break it to him, then her. She just needed to make sure he was certain about staying, that he wasn't going to end up sacrificing his life simply to act out of duty and stay for his daughter. *Or her.* That was why she'd let him go in the first place.

"You coming?"

Ben's voice from up ahead spurred her back in

to action. She urged Willy into a trot and shook her head to rid her mind of its worries.

Ben chanced a glance over his shoulder. Rebecca was sitting so elegantly on the horse it looked as though she was right at home, but he knew it had taken a lot of courage for her to get back in the saddle and open up to him. It was a weird feeling, being back out here with Rebecca. He wasn't quite sure what to do, how to act, what to say. Did he behave like they were just old friends reunited, or was he meant to factor in *that* night? Maybe it was because he'd become used to casual relationships with women; women he'd meet after a polo game, drink champagne with and then realize he had absolutely zero things in common with them. Whereas with Bec…seeing her again was like finding a favorite something that he'd missed for years, then realizing it still fit like a glove. But they were only friends, had been *only* friends for years.

He stopped at the creek's edge, no more than a trickle of water flowing down beneath some overhanging trees. It had been their spot, the place they'd always come to talk, when they needed to be alone. Parent troubles, friends, horse issues—it had been their place to figure life out.

It didn't look any different now than it had then. Ben dismounted and tied his horse loosely to a blue gum tree. He turned back around to Rebecca. She had her feet out of the stirrups, stretching her ankles, and the grimace on her face was hard to ignore.

"Every single part of my body is protesting right now," she explained.

"Want a hand down?"

Rebecca looked at him gratefully. "Oh, yeah."

He tried his hardest not to look, not to feel, but it was impossible. She swung her far leg over and came down toward him, and Ben put both hands up, catching her around the waist and guiding her to the ground. She landed with a tiny thump.

His palms were pressed against the flimsy material of her T-shirt, he could feel her taut skin beneath his hands. Despite his best intentions he didn't let go, not straight away, their bodies only inches apart. It wasn't until Rebecca cleared her throat that he stepped back, hands falling away.

Ben was about to apologize, but she turned, her dark blue eyes smiling in his direction. There was nothing to be said. The attraction that had started the night before he'd left was still there, he knew it and she knew it. But things had changed. She was a mom now, and he couldn't be a dad, not even a stepdad. And with Bec? If anything happened between them, it wasn't going to be a casual night of sex again—she meant too much for him to treat her like that. Which left him wondering what the hell *could* happen between them. If he had to consider the possibility of getting close to someone's else's kid.

"I should be saying thank you, Bec," he said, searching for the right words. "You shouldn't have lied to me, but the fact that you let me follow my dreams? You were an awesome friend. It was the best thing I've ever done and I don't regret it for a second."

She nodded, her eyes leaving his as if she was

nervous about something. "I wasn't that great a friend."

He chuckled. "Believe me, you were." She hadn't brought up that night and he wasn't going to, either, because the last thing he needed was for her to be embarrassed when things were starting to feel easy between them again. "When my mom left, there wasn't a day that went past that I didn't feel guilty. Knowing that she'd sacrificed everything she'd ever wanted to have me, it made me feel like crap. But then I guess you already know all that, right?"

Rebecca reached out, her fingers brushing his arm in the softest caress as she met his gaze again. "She had no right to make you feel that way."

Ben shrugged. "Maybe. But when you're eight years old and you find out that your mom never wanted you? It's not exactly an easy pill to swallow. No kid deserves that."

"Maybe she regretted telling you that," Rebecca said.

He ground his teeth together, trying to keep his

anger at bay. "If she regretted it she'd have come back. She made it pretty clear that her career was more important than I was."

Rebecca's hand fell away, her smile sad. "You deserved better, Ben. We both know that."

"Hey, I'm a big boy now, the past is in the past and all that," he said, brushing it off as if it meant nothing to him, even though there wasn't a day that passed that he didn't wonder how a mother could do that to her son. "All I was trying to say was I'm not angry with you, for lying to me. You let me go, and I should be thanking you instead of being so angry. You were never the kind of person to hold someone back and that makes you special."

He saw a flicker of something in her face, something he couldn't put his finger on, but he didn't call her out on it. It'd been a long time since they'd been together, so maybe he was wrong.

"Just tell me it was worth it?" she asked. "That you had the time of your life."

He bumped shoulders with her, grinning. "It

was incredible. You would have loved it over there."

She laughed. "You mean the playing and the horses, or the champagne and the parties?"

"Both. Although the latter was definitely the highlight." He laughed. "Seriously, the money over there is incredible. The champagne and top-shelf liquor flows like it's soda, and the clothes and the diamonds, the cars and horseflesh, it's like nothing I'd ever seen before. I never got used to it, even after all that time, and I'm sure as hell pleased I never tried to keep up with those lifestyles."

"Sounds tough. You must have been so miserable," she joked.

"Yeah, it was such a bore riding hundred-thousand-dollar horses and swilling Veuve Clicquot."

"Hmm, I'm sure."

This was what he'd missed, just hanging out with someone he actually had a connection with. Playing overseas had been fun, but this was real life, and it was reality that he'd yearned for. Telling stories about his time was fun, but in truth it had been superficial, and he was happy to have his feet back on Australian soil, even if he still missed his teammates like crazy.

"So tell me all about it. Was it as amazing as we always thought it would be? Parties aside?"

Rebecca toyed with the frayed hem of her T-shirt and watched Ben skim stones across the water. He was lying down, propped up by one elbow, while she sat cross-legged beside him. Telling him the truth had been tough, but after hearing him say she'd done the right thing, listening to him talk about his mom again, she was feeling better about what she'd kept from him. He was still going to be furious when she told him everything, but at least they'd made some headway.

"Yeah. But the guys are rough." He grimaced. "As in rough with their horses. It's just the way things are with polo, but you know how I am. I love the sport, but I missed home." Ben looked off into the distance. "I gotta say that it was the first time I'd ever felt like part of a real family, though, so that was good. I mean, Gus always remained the most important person in my life, but feeling like I had a whole team of brothers was pretty cool. We traveled in the owner's private jets around the world to play. He even jetted the horses rather than keep different stables. The money he had was surreal."

She wondered if he'd missed her, or if he was just referring to Gus. Or maybe he meant the red Australian dirt and she was being way too sentimental. Either way, what he'd experienced sounded incredible.

"You know, it was like, every day over there was a way to prove to myself that I was worth something. I wanted to show Gus that I could dream big and achieve what I'd always talked about, but maybe it was a way to prove to the rest of the world that I didn't deserve to be orphaned by my parents."

Rebecca nodded. "I get it." She'd always known he was running from demons, because she'd always been the one he opened up to.

"And how about you? You pleased you stayed behind in the end?" He shook his head. "Or did you regret what had happened?"

"I should have told you I didn't make the team."

"Yeah, but the question is did you actually want to go or not?" he asked, his expression serious. "Was it still what you wanted?"

"To start with, yes. But after my fall? It killed my confidence, Ben. I wanted to go away, but I couldn't just head off and expect to tag along with you if I wasn't playing or working. I needed to figure out what the hell I was going to do with my life, find something that I could actually make a go of." He kept flicking the stones, listening but not saying anything, so she continued. "I should have been better at emailing, but then I had Lexie and..." She didn't know what else to say.

"I get it. You were busy, times changed. It wasn't like we were together or anything." He angled his body so he was facing her, a frown dragging his mouth down. "But what happened that night, it was a long time coming, right?"

She sucked in a breath. "Um, yeah." Rebecca glanced at Ben, his expression serious. "But we always said we'd never ruin things, didn't we? That our friendship was what mattered."

A slow smile spread across Ben's face. "Maybe we were stupid. Maybe we should have just followed our instincts from the start."

"I thought our instincts were to be friends and not complicate things," she said drily.

"Yeah, well look how well that turned out." Ben reached out and touched her hand, a gesture that shouldn't have rattled her but did. "And then you went and met someone else and had a baby."

Her heart started to pound, as if it was about to beat right out of her chest.

"You okay?"

She nodded. "Just thinking about Lexie. I only ever leave her if I have to go to work, so I'm feeling a bit guilty."

"She's with your parents, though?"

"Yeah. They adore her and she has them wrapped around her little finger." Bec laughed.

"She probably has more fun with them than she has with me, but I still don't like leaving her."

She looked across into a pair of deep brown eyes that were hauntingly, yet comfortingly, the exact same as her daughter's, the gold fleck unmistakable.

"You sure you're not going to tell me who the guy was? Because if he's someone I know..."

Rebecca gave Ben a smile that could have won her an acting award, a practiced smile to stop him from worrying. She'd been using the same one on her dad for years. "How about we pretend like we've gone back in time for the rest of the afternoon?"

He grunted. "I just wish I'd been here for you, that's all. You shouldn't have had to go through that alone."

"As my friend?" she asked, pulse hammering again. "You wish you were here for me as my friend or something else?"

He looked confused. "Of course. That's what we were, right?"

His words hurt. Like a fist to her gut. He might

not have thought they were together, that they'd become anything more than good friends, but that night they had spent together had changed everything for her. She'd fallen in love with him, and if she was honest, it wasn't as though she'd ever fallen back out of love. Not once in all these years, even after meeting plenty of nice guys through the restaurant. But even if he'd stayed, they may have just gone back to being friends, to nothing more. Unless of course she'd told him about her being pregnant, then he'd have probably proposed to her because of his sense of duty. And the only thing worse than wishing they were together would have been knowing they were together because he thought they had to be.

"We *were* friends," she said, sucking back a burst of emotion that he would probably never understand. "But I was fine, Ben. I was absolutely fine."

"I guess being a mom kept you pretty busy. I just hope you were happy and busy."

Ben said it with a smile but all Rebecca felt was a lump of dread knot in her throat. Lexie. Her daughter. *Their daughter.* She needed to change the subject before they broached into even more dangerous territory, or before Ben started to figure out the timeline.

"Bec?"

Ben looked worried. She closed her eyes for a moment and felt the sun trickle through the branches above her. Her feet were hot inside her boots, but the rest of her felt great. Bare arms in the sun, the sticky air brushing past her skin, and nothing but the sound of birds cawing in the trees. She owed it to herself to relax, and if she stopped worrying, then maybe it wouldn't be so hard to change the subject and just enjoy being with Ben as she tried to figure everything out.

"You know what?" she said, her eyes lazily popping open. "Let's just lie here a bit longer. I never get to sit and do nothing anymore."

A little part of her might feel like the world's worst mother for being here and leaving Lexie at home, but it was once in more than three years, and if she kept working at the pace she did every day for another year, she'd probably end up in hospital with exhaustion.

"Fine by me," said Ben, pulling his cap lower over his eyes and reclining back.

They were side by side now, so close to touching, but achingly far apart. Rebecca had closed her eyes again, but her body was far from relaxed. She wanted to tell Ben how good this felt, to be here with him again, to forget about everything else. She wanted to tell him she'd missed him, that she wanted to be part of his life again, but she knew it was impossible. She wished she could explain why she'd done what she'd done, how she hadn't felt worthy of him, how she hadn't wanted to hold him back from his dreams, but nothing sounded quite right when she practiced it in her mind.

If she was truly honest with herself, she knew that coming here had been a mistake. She had known it from the day Gus had asked her to make the trip. But if she hadn't come, she would always have been wondering what if. What if Ben wanted to see her for a reason? What if Gus died and she felt guilty forever for not making the effort to see him? The list in her mind just went on and on.

And now that she was here, it was intoxicating. The smell, feel, touch of horses beneath her hands and around her were enough to lull her back in time. The same with Ben. The house. Gus, too. It was like being transported back to enjoy a time where everything seemed fine, where anything she dreamed was possible, where being with Ben was a possibility.

As if he knew she was thinking about him, Ben nudged his hat back and propped himself up on his elbow again. Rebecca had opened her eyes as soon as he had moved, but she stayed lying on her back.

"You ever think what would have happened if I hadn't gone away?"

Rebecca let out a low lungful of air and looked over at him. He seemed to have moved closer but she knew he hadn't. Ben was plucking at some long shoots of grass, but she could tell he was off balance, that he wasn't entirely comfortable talking to her about the past, although she guessed he'd been sitting on that question awhile.

"Yeah, I do." She took a slow, deep breath. "Or at least I used to. A lot."

They stayed silent for a moment, both looking at his hands, watching his fingers pull at each blade. Rebecca's mouth was dry, as if she'd just consumed a ball of cotton wool. He had no idea how much she wished he'd stayed, how often she thought of how different life would be. For starters, she wouldn't be a single mom, because she'd have told him right from the start. The *only* reason she'd kept it from him was so she wasn't the one responsible for killing his dream because she hadn't wanted him to resent her or her child. *Especially not their child.*

"So what was your conclusion?"

Rebecca felt her cheeks flush hot. What had her thoughts been?

"I think we'd have made it," he said, not waiting for her to reply. "If we'd just admitted how we felt instead of pretending like it meant nothing. If we'd been together instead of pretending like we were only supposed to be friends when we both know that was crap."

Ben maneuvered the single blade of grass between forefinger and thumb, before lifting it to run it over her bare arm. She couldn't stop her eyes from closing, the tiny hairs on her arm rising with the touch, her breath coming in short pants. It felt as though he was caressing her, skin to skin, even though no part of him was actually touching her, the grass doing all the skimming across her arm.

Her eyes popped open again when he spoke, but she was feeling drowsy and excited all at once. Her mind roaring, stomach turning.

"Why did it take us so long to realize?" he asked, voice sexy and low.

She knew exactly what he meant. After all those years of being buddies, friends only, why had it taken an alcohol-fueled night and him leaving to draw them together? When they could have had so long having fun instead of pretending like they both just wanted to be platonic. But the very next day they'd gone on like *nothing* had happened.

"We could have been great," she croaked, still entranced by the grass-to-skin thing he was doing to her.

He stopped then, and their eyes met. She leaned in, her gaze falling from his mouth back to his eyes. Was he trying to tell her he still wanted her? Was he trying to tell her that their night together hadn't been one big mistake?

"Rebecca, I..."

She watched him expectantly, desperate for him to close the gap between them and move forward. Aching to taste his kiss. After all this time of wishing he was with her, that he would come home for her, and now he was so close.

Ben looked at her long and hard before reaching one hand into her hair, cupping the back of her skull and drawing her close. He crushed her lips so softly against his, the light touch of his skin sending ripples of pleasure down her spine. It should have felt wrong, but if felt so, so right.

Ben ran his hand down the length of her hair, before pulling back and looking at her, his smile crinkling his eyes in that delicious way it always did. The Ben she'd said goodbye to had had no little fine wrinkles, hardly any stubble on his jaw, but she liked him ever better this way than before. There was a maturity there that she found achingly attractive, shorter hair and a covering of barely there facial hair.

How was it that some men just got more and more delicious with age? He'd been handsome as a teen, all the women had liked him in his early twenties, especially in his polo getup, but now he was a man. Grown-up. Strong. *Real*. The kind of man you knew could protect you and rescue you, like a modern-day warrior who looked after those close to him. She could look into those dark brown eyes all day long and never tire of the view. And those lips…*mmm*, she loved those lips.

"I've really missed you, Bec. And I don't just mean that I've missed my friend. I've wanted you ever since that night."

She nodded, biting down on her lower lip. And she could spend all day listening to words like that.

He gave her a heartbreaking smile, then lay

back again, his eyes toward the sky. She loved that about him, too. The way he could say something like that and not worry about hearing the words back. Confident enough in himself to say what he thought and leave it at that.

She watched him lying there and wondered what he was thinking about. Things had changed from old friends reunited to something more, and despite loving every second of that kiss, she was terrified. Alarm bells she should have been listening to were trying their hardest to signal, but she pushed them away. The bubble was going to burst soon, she was only delaying the inevitable, because as much as Ben was saying he liked her as a whole lot more than just friends now, when he found out what she'd kept from him he'd never forgive her. *Never.*

CHAPTER SIX

"HOW ARE YOU FEELING?"

Rebecca cast her eye over Ben. She would be feeling a whole lot better if she wasn't staring at his lips and wishing he was kissing her all over again.

"I think I'll be stiff tomorrow."

He laughed, a deep chuckle that made Rebecca tingle all over.

"Maybe dinner will make you feel better?"

Dinner? "You mean just here?"

He adjusted his baseball cap, one hand on the reins. "Gus thought we'd go out for dinner, just somewhere local, nothing fancy."

She nodded. If it was the three of them, then she had nothing to worry about.

"I've missed good Australian food. Prawns, Moreton Bay bugs, baramundi…" Ben blew out a whistle. "Man, I'm starving just thinking about all that seafood."

"I eat at our restaurant all the time, but I'm usually just standing out back having a few mouthfuls when I get a chance."

"So you don't get out much?"

"Nope." She grinned. "My girl is my life, and unless it's a burger or somewhere with a playground we tend to stay at home unless it's work."

Ben was riding close to her, but the horses didn't seem to mind. Rebecca was worried about bumping knees or stirrups. Kind of the same worry she remembered as a teen anticipating her first kiss, not wanting to knock teeth and knowing it was going to happen anyway.

"You're a great mom, Bec," Ben said with a smile. "But you deserve a night out and I need the company."

She could tell by the look on his face that he wasn't just saying it.

"How would you know that I'm any good as a mom?"

"Because I can see it in you. You've always been

so caring, so gentle, I just know you'd be fantastic." He laughed. "Maybe that's why I knew we'd never work out, because I need to find some troubled woman who's as screwed up as me about kids. You were always going to make a great mom."

She looked down, but when she eventually raised her eyes he was still watching her. His eyes flickered from the track they were riding to sideways, catching her as they passed. Every time he said something like that, every little comment where he was trying to flatter her or just plain make up for the fact that nothing had happened between them, it just made her resolve to tell him waver.

"So you're still sure about that? That you'll never be a father?" The words were almost impossible to push out, but she did it. "I always thought you'd, I don't know, grow out of it or something."

"Hell yes, I'm still sure," he said straight back, not missing a beat. "I'm not dad material. Never have been, never will be."

"But you're so different to your mom, you're..."

"Not going to be a dad." His tone was final, determined. "I can't be. I like being around kids, but I can't be the dad."

Rebecca shrugged. "I just know you'd be amazing, that's all."

"Well don't eye me up as your next baby daddy, okay?" he said with a chuckle. "Because it's never gonna happen. I'll be the fun uncle to your little one and that's as close as I'll get."

Ben was laughing but Rebecca could hardly breathe, let alone joke back. Her head was pounding as loud as her heart now.

"Bec?"

She forced a smile.

"Man, I'm sorry. I didn't mean that, you know, like you'd want another baby with a different guy…"

"Ben, it's fine, you were just joking around," she said. "Now tell me where we're going for dinner."

"Everything okay at home?"

Ben reached out to touch Bec's arm, realizing he'd frightened her. She'd jumped the minute he'd spoken.

"Yeah, everything's fine."

"So you're not about to run off back to the city on me?" he asked.

"Ha, not yet. But I've never actually been away from her before, not properly, so I might bail on you in the night. I'm usually back from the restaurant by 1 a.m. and then I crash wherever she is."

They both laughed, but Ben guessed she was telling the truth. "So I have this crazy feeling that your dating pool must be pretty limited."

The shock on Bec's face was palpable. "Yeah, I guess you could say that."

"Sorry, none of my business. I just mean that between working the hours you do and being a mom..." He ran a hand through his hair, wishing he'd just kept his mouth shut. "Sorry, just forget I said anything. I seem to be getting pretty good at putting my foot in it."

Bec sighed, her chest visibly rising as she took a big breath to fill her lungs again. "Since I had

Lexie, I haven't really dated at all. The last few years have just flown past, one blur to another."

Ben watched her face, tried to read whether he'd offended her or not, and got the feeling it was definitely the latter. "I guess what I'm trying to ask is whether you're seeing anyone right now."

The question hung between them, the silence almost painful as she stared at him, her mouth open but not moving.

"Ah, no. No I'm not," she stammered.

"Good." He grinned, moving closer to her, every part of him focused on every single part of her, her skin warm beneath his touch as he circled his fingers around her wrist, his other hand rising to her face. "Then you won't mind if I do this again."

Bec was still silent, but she hadn't tried to move away, either, so he followed his instincts and did what he should have done over a decade ago when they'd first met. He'd always been so conscious of not ruining their friendship, of not pushing her and waiting to let her make the first move if she wanted things to change between them, but not now. Now he knew exactly what he wanted, and tonight that something was Bec. All thoughts aside, he wanted Rebecca.

When they'd been together last time, they'd been drunk. Right now, it was still daylight, he could see every expression on her face. Ben didn't hesitate any longer; he cupped her cheek and kissed her, lips closing over hers gently at first, testing the waters, then more firmly as she leaned into him. He kissed her just like he'd wanted to kiss her the four years he'd been away, stroking her hair, inhaling the feminine scent of her perfume. Her lips were warm and pliable, so soft that he forced himself to slow down, to tease her and be gentle with her.

Ben stifled a groan as she placed her hands on his chest, pushing him back ever so slightly, but enough that their lips parted. He stared down into eyes the most beautiful shade of blue, watched as her breath came in short, ragged pants.

"Slow down, cowboy," she murmured.

"Slow down?" He chuckled and leaned in,

pressing another kiss to her lips even as she tried to push him away. "I've been waiting a real long time to do that again, so I'm kinda keen to speed things up."

Rebecca laughed, eyes locked on his as they stood still. It was as though everything else had disappeared and it was just the two of them—Ben wanted her, he always had. The only trouble now was that he had to make it clear to her that he wasn't looking for a role as stepdad of the year.

"I'm not sure we should be doing this," she muttered.

Ben shrugged. "Why not?"

"Because we've already made this mistake once."

"Maybe it wasn't a mistake," he said simply. "Are you sure it wasn't the right thing, only we did it at the wrong time?"

Rebecca looked unsure. "I can't commit to anything, Ben. It's just not that simple for me anymore."

"Then let's just keep it simple," he said. The thought of being around her daughter wasn't something he was sure about, only because he didn't know what to do around kids, but he missed Bec, and he wanted his friend back.

"What are you suggesting?" she asked, eyes wide as she clutched the front of his T-shirt.

"How about we take it one night at a time." Ben wanted her so badly—in his arms, in his bed, hell, he just wanted Bec back in his life again. He knew things were never going to be the same, but still.

"What about if it was just for tonight?" she asked.

Ben hated the thought of only having her for one night, but one night might lead to more and... to hell with it. One night was better than nothing, and he had plenty of time to convince her otherwise.

"Whatever you want, Bec." Ben ran his hands up and down her arms, his body humming with anticipation. "You set the rules and I'll follow."

She smiled up at him. "Slow. Just keep it slow, and you won't hear any complaints from me."

He laughed. "Okay, well in the interests of

keeping things slow, I'm gonna go do a few jobs before we head out. You okay here?"

Rebecca nodded, taking a step back, her arms folded across her chest. They stood, watching each other for a moment; a moment where Ben could have said to hell with it and stormed back toward her again, but he didn't. Because he didn't want to scare Bec off, not before their night together had even started.

Rebecca wasn't sure if she was being fobbed off, or if he actually had some things to do, but she didn't mind. Still obsessing about *the kiss*, but fine. She was bound to find something to keep her entertained for the next while. With foals to watch and horses being trained, there wasn't any shortage of things to do. And it would at least keep her thoughts pure. No more sizing Ben up as if he was a juicy steak waiting to be consumed. Or maybe that's exactly what she needed to do—get him out of her system once and for all. Although maybe that's essentially what she'd just agreed to.

"I'll take your bag up to the house and leave it just inside the door. Make yourself at home, okay?" Ben called over his shoulder.

"Sounds good. Thanks." It was as if they hadn't just had that whole awkward conversation, as if things were back to normal again.

She'd dropped her small case to the ground and Ben bent to retrieve it. Rebecca almost reached out to touch his hair—as thick as Lexie's and almost the same color.

"I'll see you soon."

Ben nodded, his mouth twisted into a smile, and turned, her bag in his hand. She just stood there, watching him go, and wondered what the hell she was doing playing along as if nothing had changed. But despite wanting to look away, Rebecca's eyes were locked on the way his jeans hung from his wry hips, his tanned arms seemingly chocolate against his white T, and the way his stride ate up the dirt as he walked.

She was in way over her head just being back at McFarlane's, but she was damned if she was going to do anything about it until at least the morning. Lexie was safe, she was enjoying herself, or at least trying to, and the surroundings were breathtaking. Not to mention she wanted a good catch-up with Gus, too. *And maybe a repeat evening with Ben.*

Once Ben disappeared around the corner, so she knew there was no chance of being caught, she wandered back over to the yards. It was as if the filly was beckoning her, only she knew it was plain stupid to even think like that. The horse was probably just grazing, minding her own business, but Rebecca felt a pull toward the yard. She reasoned with herself that it was perhaps just because she felt confident after the ride, but there was something else there. She wanted to prove that she still had it, that after submerging herself in motherhood, and everything else life had thrown her way, that she could still change, go back in time. Be the one person to make a difference and connect with an animal and develop their trust. The only problem was that she wanted to find out alone, without the pressure of anyone watching. She hadn't lied to Ben when she'd said her fall and everything that had happened had broken her—her confidence had been in tatters and it had taken a long time for her to claw back from her despair.

Her feet walked her over in the right direction but her mind was screaming out to just head back to the house and read a book. Anything but put herself in a position of potential danger with a half-wild horse. Something about being here was making her feel like the fifteen-year-old who'd first visited the farm, full of confidence and not planning on letting anything stop her from fulfilling her dreams.

Missy was watching her, although she was pretending not to. Her head was bent down, but one eye was focused on Rebecca's progress. She ignored the horse, keeping her gaze focused on a spot to the side, not wanting to threaten her. This was about the animal deciding to trust her, and direct eye contact established nothing but dominance.

Rebecca looked over each shoulder but no one was around. She walked slowly until she reached the corral, then cautiously bent to maneuver through the railings. She was still wondering what the hell she was doing but she was in there now.

The horse looked incredibly beautiful. The sunlight was bouncing off her shiny black coat, brown dapples ever so delicately showing through. Everything about the filly was immaculate, from her trimmed tail to her glossy mane, and it made Rebecca think she had to be pretty special. There was a reason Gus wanted to persist with her.

"Hey, girl," she called, keeping her voice soft. It was hard not to sound nervous but she was trying her best. She knew the horse would have already picked up on her heartbeat, and she needed to slow down.

The horse snorted but kept grazing, unworried. Rebecca felt a familiar static in her stomach but forced herself to keep on going. This was her chance to see if she still had it. She seriously doubted it.

"You and me," she half whispered, "we're going to be good friends."

Rebecca stopped and waited. The horse still didn't look up. She decided to change her tactic.

Missy was still watching her, but Rebecca didn't acknowledge it. Instead, she sat down, careful to move slowly, crossing her legs and keeping her head down. She kept her eyes focused on the ground. Looking up, even slightly, would break the connection, break the trust, and make the horse look at her as a predator rather than a nonthreatening being. Now it was time to wait.

Sure enough, it was only minutes before the horse decided to investigate. Rebecca stayed still. It seemed dangerous, but she knew that so long as she was nonthreatening and didn't spook her, there was little chance of injury.

It was nerve-racking, sitting so still, but she did it. Missy had her head low to the ground, looking at Rebecca, snorting. She moved forward slowly, inquisitively, and soon her muzzle was touching Rebecca. Just gently, her whiskers skimming the very top of her head, moving her hair ever so, blowing through her nostrils close to Rebecca's skin.

And then she sniffed at her face, tentatively, and Rebecca couldn't help but smile. It had taken this incredibly untrusting horse just minutes to come close, and now she was standing, unworried, beside her. A horse Ben claimed hadn't developed a bond with any of the men, not even him.

Rebecca raised her eyes, still not making direct contact. A flutter ran through her veins. *She still had it.* Like clockwork, the horse stayed calm, brought her nose close to Rebecca's, and Bec slowly reached out one hand. It was magical, as if there was an element of witchcraft, but Rebecca knew that sometimes a horse just needed a gentle approach, and sometimes preferred a woman over a man.

She touched her gently, then drew her feet up beneath her, until she was in a squat position.

"You're a good girl, Missy," she clucked. "A real good girl."

The horse had her ears pricked, listening. But she was no longer nervous, or afraid.

Rebecca reluctantly pulled up to her full height, one hand still resting on Missy's shoulder.

"I think you and I are going to get along just fine."

Now she was standing beside the horse, running her hand rhythmically back and forward along her soft coat. Rebecca loved the senses of being back around horses. The smell, touch, feel, everything just took her on a path back in time. It didn't mean she felt confident about getting *on* them, but maybe handling them was different. She still felt an element of control that she hadn't realized she'd still have.

"Well done."

Gus's croaky tone took her by surprise. She stayed still, not letting it break her bond with the horse.

She eventually turned around, keeping one hand on Missy, and was surprised to see Gus and Ben both standing nearby, watching her. Her face flooded with heat, embarrassed that they'd been there when she'd thought she was alone.

"Nice work," said Ben.

Rebecca could tell from the look on his face that he was pleased with her. His eyes were shining, a big smile stretching his face wide.

"I knew you had it in you still," said Gus, his focus on the filly. "I knew."

Rebecca looked between the two men. Ben was like a replica of his granddad—just a young, stronger version. They both had the same magnetism, the same aura about them, and she loved them both dearly, no matter how much she tried to pretend otherwise.

"You set me up." She said her words in an even, calm voice to avoid alarming the horse. "You guys knew I wouldn't be able to resist her and I walked straight into the trap."

The two men looked at one another and smiled. The kind of coconspirator type of smile she remembered only too well. She had been prey to their duping plenty of times as a gullible teenager.

"Maybe," Ben called out. "But I bet you feel damn good for doing it."

She tried to look angry and failed miserably, not really caring what they'd done. They'd been right—it made her feel good for proving to herself that she could still do it, because lately all she did was work in the restaurant. And if she wasn't working she was caring for Lexie. It was nice to know she was still good at something else.

"I'd say you really owe me that dinner now," she said.

Gus hobbled off with his cane, whistling a familiar tune. She knew he was pleased with himself. He wouldn't have doubted for a moment that she could resist the filly, but then he hadn't known how low she'd been, what had really happened.

Ben grinned at her and Rebecca almost felt she'd be safer staying in the round pen than being beside him. He was definitely more mature than she remembered him, and with that came a certain confidence that she didn't recall. The way he looked at her, it made her feel wanted, that he appreciated her. For two people who were meant to be friends, it was most unnerving. But then hadn't they just agreed that they both wanted to be more than just platonic, for tonight anyway?

"I'm looking forward to it," she muttered, more to herself than for anyone else's ears.

She watched his eyes as they danced over her. A delicious, deep brown that was dangerous yet kind. This was a man she trusted, that she had loved and still did, but every time she looked at him, there was an echo of guilt that she couldn't truly shake. If he ever found out what she'd kept from him, she knew he'd never look at her that way again. Which was why she had to let herself have this one night with him before she sent everything into free fall. Her telling the truth wasn't just going to affect Ben, it was going to impact on her own family, and Gus. She'd lied to them all, and after keeping her secret for so long…it wasn't even worth thinking about what might happen.

Ben was still watching her and she shook away

the worries and focused on the filly again. She could enjoy the next day and night; beyond that she had no idea what was going to happen.

CHAPTER SEVEN

BEN SAT ON the wide veranda that stretched around three sides of the big old house, beer in hand, mind a million miles away. The low early evening sun drifted in through the thick wisteria, and he closed his eyes, basking in the quiet peacefulness of his surroundings.

There was something about Australia, something he couldn't explain, but being back was better than good, it felt right. He thought he'd never come back, but after a few years it was all he'd wanted. He'd always craved a family; even though he had Gus it hadn't been like growing up with parents and siblings, and his polo family had given him a team load of brothers to live and travel with. But now…now he wanted to be home, was ready to be home. And the only thing he wanted more was Rebecca. His only trouble was exactly *what* he wanted from her. One second he thought he knew, and the next he was questioning himself all over again.

Ben took another pull of beer and lazily opened his eyes. Rebecca was upstairs getting ready for dinner and he was just biding his time waiting for her. His grandfather had told him with a big grin that he was tired and turning in early, which he knew was rubbish, but he wasn't going to argue with him. He wanted some time alone with Bec, just the two of them. He only wished he had his head in the right place first. All he knew was he wanted her, and beyond that he didn't have a clue what he was going to do.

He heard a noise and finished his beer, jumped up and opened the side door that led back into the house. And then he saw Rebecca, making her way down the stairs, wearing tight jeans that showed off every inch of her super long legs, and a sparkly sequined top that seemed to make her eyes shine an even brighter shade of blue when she came closer. She was a knockout, pure and simple. All the women put together from the fancy polo days couldn't hold a candle to her.

"Wow," said Ben, realizing she was staring at him. "You look great." *She looked better than great, she looked freaking amazing.*

Rebecca's cheeks flushed. "Thanks."

He glanced up and down her body again, quickly, hoping she wouldn't notice. All this time he'd wondered if he was imagining how beautiful she was, but his answer was right there in front of him.

"No, seriously, Bec, you look stunning."

She looked self-conscious, slipping her jacket on and covering up far too much skin for his liking.

"So where are we going? You still haven't told me."

Ben glanced down at his shirt with the sleeves rolled up and his worn pair of jeans. Maybe he should have gotten more dressed up.

"Somewhere good. Let's go."

"What about Gus?"

"He's missing in action." Ben laughed. "Looks

like he set us both up. Crazy old fool made the booking the day you said you were coming, then scurried off to bed just before as if he had the whole thing planned from the beginning."

He liked the fact that Rebecca still blushed. She might be all grown-up and a mom, but she was still shy when it came to anything happening beyond friends between them and it was an endearing quality. Especially after how bold so many of the women he'd met overseas had been, how brazen they'd been about wanting to bed any of the guys in his team.

"So it's just the two of us, then?"

"That okay with you?" he asked.

"Just two old friends catching up, right?"

Ben caught her wink and gave her a quiet smile straight back. He owed Gus a huge thank-you for giving him some alone time with Bec, and he wasn't going to waste a minute.

"You ready?"

"As I'll ever be. Let's go."

Ben grabbed his keys off the hall stand and checked he had his wallet in his back pocket, before touching his hand to Rebecca's back and guiding her toward the front door.

They pulled up outside Ruby's restaurant and Rebecca ran her hands over her jeans and gave herself a mental pep talk. She only had a moment alone before Ben moved around to open her door. It was funny, she never expected men to be quite so chivalrous when it came to everyday things like that, but opening doors was just the kind of thing Ben had always done.

"Not quite like our old haunt."

Ben had laughter in his eyes and Bec grinned.

"Nothing like it," she affirmed. They'd had a favorite burger place back in the day, when they'd been able to eat as much grease as they wanted and still be skinny as racehorses.

"You sure you don't want to jump back in the car and get a burger? Maybe some fries drowned in ketchup?"

Rebecca shook her head and felt relieved that she'd loosened up a little. It had been silly worrying, there was nothing to feel concerned about.

Whatever happened, happened. She could worry about everything else another day. She needed to give herself a break, even if it was for only a few hours.

"I think this place looks like exactly where we should be headed. It'll be nice to be waited on for once."

Ben walked beside her as they crossed the short distance to the restaurant. It was nothing too fancy, not like some of the Melbourne restaurants she encountered in the city, but it was fresh and modern, and the food smelled great. She liked that she could partially see into the kitchen at the other end of the restaurant—she loved seeing the hustle and bustle of where her food was being prepared.

There was a lovely community feeling in Geelong, and it was something Rebecca missed in the city. It wasn't for everyone, but she kind of liked that if you lived here you would more than likely know a handful of the people dining. That the waiters would know you by name because this was your favorite local dinner spot.

As if on cue a waiter appeared, dressed in black with a smart white half apron tied at his waist.

"Ben," said the man, nodding. "Nice to see you back again so soon."

Rebecca felt her back bristle and wished it away, wondering if Ben had been here with a date already since he'd been home.

"The food was too good to bother going anywhere else," Ben replied politely.

The waiter motioned for them to follow, menus in hand, and Ben placed his open palm lightly to her back again. It wasn't any less surprising than the first time he'd done it, but she managed to gulp down her nerves.

She glanced around the room, seeing mostly couples and a few bigger tables. It was nice—intimate but not fussy, just how she liked it. And it was only early so the place wasn't too busy yet.

The waiter stopped and placed the menus on a table overlooking the water, one of only a few in the restaurant. Either Ben had fluked a good spot, or that crafty old grandfather of his had planned the whole night! She was pretty sure there was no luck involved, which only made her nervous all over again.

"I'll be back to take your drink order soon."

Ben waited for Rebecca to sit before taking his jacket off and settling down across from her. He cleared his throat. Rebecca raised her eyes from the water glass she'd been focused on, trying to quell the nerves jingling like chimes in her belly. It was stupid to feel so unsure, they had way too much history for her to even think about being uncomfortable just chatting and sharing a meal with him, but she couldn't help the way she felt.

"I, ah, didn't exactly plan this," Ben said, eyebrows drawn together as if he was trying to figure out how to explain the fact they had the most romantic table in the house.

"Oh, don't worry!" Rebecca tried to take her voice down a decibel from the high-pitched soprano it had altered to. "This is fine. It's lovely. Maybe Gus did it just to embarrass you."

The waiter reappeared and Ben selected a white wine from the famous Barossa Valley. Rebecca felt like chugging a whole bottle just to calm herself, although thankfully she had the menu to scan now, which meant she had something to look at other than Ben or the gorgeous view.

"What are you going to have?" Ben had placed his down on the table and was watching her.

"Me, ah, well…maybe fish of the day. I love the sound of the king prawns that come with it."

He nodded. "Hmm, good choice. I've been hanging out for seafood so I'm thinking the Moreton Bay bugs and prawns."

They ordered and Rebecca was left with no other option but to look back at Ben. It terrified her. Apart from the similarity of those eyes to Lexie's, she was scared of the intensity of his stare, of the way his eyes looked at her as if they could see right to her soul. Maybe that was why she'd never been attracted to another man since Ben had left. Once she'd had those eyes on her, no other pair ever lived up to it.

"You never did tell me what your parents are up to. What about your brother?"

Phew, she was happy talking family. Safe topic. She was just pleased Ben hadn't run into her brother himself, because then they'd have bonded over their mutual desire to know who Lexie's father was, which would only make the whole situation worse when she did finally come clean.

"Mum and Dad are great, they're making the most of retirement," she said, gratefully taking a gulp of wine. "They spend a bit of time traveling, and I'm happy running the restaurant. It means I can spend lots of time with Lexie, but it does make juggling things tough when they head away on one of their cruises."

Ben nodded and leaned back in his chair. Rebecca almost felt the tiny bit of extra distance made it easier for her to relax, and at least she knew Ben was genuinely interested in her family. It had almost broken her own mom's heart when he'd left—she'd absolutely loved him and the feeling had been mutual, even more so probably because Ben had zero relationship with his own mother.

"My brother, well, he's a dad now, another on the way. Met a great girl through work and they've been together and happy ever since. But they have twins, so Lexie is always trying to compete with them and keep up with their adventures."

"What about you?" Ben asked, leaning forward. "Have you been okay, really? I mean, I know you love your daughter, but it must have been pretty tough doing it alone. Growing up so quick like that, aside from all the other stuff you went through."

Rebecca felt a mist cloud her eyes but she expertly blinked it away. She didn't cry, it just wasn't what she did. And this was no exception, just because someone had actually asked her that question and genuinely cared about the answer. She wished she could just tell him, that she could open up about what had happened and he'd open his arms wide and tell her she had nothing to worry about, that everything would miraculously be okay. But she was a realist, and she knew there was no amount of wishing that could turn what had happened into them being a happy little white-picket-fence family. If that was the case, she'd have told him right at the start when she'd first found out; if she had even a niggle of doubt that he was interested in being with her and playing happy families, then she would have told him a thousand times over.

"It's been hard, I'm not going to lie," she admitted. "But honestly? I love my girl and I like being in the restaurant, so life's pretty good. I might have given you a different answer when I was sleep deprived and exhausted a year or so ago, but I've found my rhythm now."

She knew what he wanted to know, though. Whether she'd had a man in her life, if she'd been alone all this time. There was a steely glint in his eye, a determined edge to his smile that told her he wanted to dig deeper.

"And Lexie's dad? He's never helped you out? Never been a part of her life at all?"

Rebecca reached for her wine again. This was not a conversation that she wanted to have right now. Not saying anything was one thing, but lying was something entirely different and she wasn't comfortable with it, not for a second. If she could just find the words to tell him, the right way to break it to him…

"How about you?" she asked, drawing on all her strength, not ready, not prepared enough to come out and say it yet. "You sure you don't have some gorgeous Argentinian woman packing her things as we speak to come live the good life in Australia with you?"

Their dinner arrived then and Rebecca smiled her thanks at the waiter, pleased for the distraction. Any break in the intensity of talking like this with Ben was a welcome one.

"You know what? You're the only person I've seen since coming home, other than Gus really." Ben took a mouthful and waited till he'd finished before continuing. "I just feel like I've missed out on so much time with Gus, and any time I miss out on now seems wasted." He cleared his throat, glancing up at the same time as one side of his mouth kicked out into a smile. "And no, there's no special someone. You think I would have kissed you if there was?"

Rebecca was pleased she'd already swallowed,

otherwise she'd have choked. "Ah, well…" Talk about stunning her into speechlessness. "I guess not."

"Which means we're both single."

"I guess you're right." She had control of her voice now, her nerves settling into a more sedate ball than the writhing one they'd leaped into before.

"So back to Gus," she said, refocusing on her food and cutting the fish into a more manageable bite. "Have the doctors said how long?" she asked gently.

Ben toyed with his fork, the humor that had been in his gaze fading. "Maybe six months, maybe longer, but there's nothing they can do for him. He kept it pretty quiet, but I knew when he finally came out and told me that we were on borrowed time."

"He was great to us, wasn't he?" said Rebecca, smiling at Ben even though she knew it probably hurt like hell for him to talk about his granddad like this. "I don't think either of us would have turned out the same without him. He's a one in a million kind of man."

Ben smiled back at her, his eyes locking on hers, not giving her a moment to look away. She knew he felt the same—hell, his granddad had been the only stable thing in his life, the one person who'd unconditionally loved him from the day he was born.

"He's definitely one in a million," Ben said, grinning as he watched her. "And I'm gonna spend every damn minute I can with him so he knows it."

"Well, good." She ate another mouthful, looking out at the water as she chewed. It was a beautiful balmy Melbourne night, and with the water twinkling under the soft lights, she could have been anywhere in the world. Ben might terrify her, but she also felt a pull toward him that was impossible to deny.

"Rebecca, the way I left, the way things went down between us before…"

"Don't," she said softly, interrupting him. "We

don't need to talk about it. We've already been there."

He shook his head and reached for her hand, his fingers closing over hers in a touch so gentle, so caring, it made the tiny hairs on her arm stand on end. He squeezed, forcing her to look up instead of stare at where their skin was connected, his brown eyes focused on hers.

"I don't want you to think it was because I didn't care about you," he said simply. "What happened between us was years of pent-up attraction I reckon, and maybe if I hadn't been about to fly out it would never have happened. Maybe we never would have made that leap into dangerous territory."

"Yeah," she agreed. "It was like as soon as we knew you were going, all bets were off."

He touched her cheek, his palm so soft to her face it made her sigh. "I wanted you for so long, Bec. You have no idea how hard it was for me to just keep things between us as friends. But I always knew I'd rather have you as my friend than lose you completely, so I never pushed it."

She laughed, shaking her head. “Oh, I know.”

He arched an eyebrow and only made her laugh louder. “Then why the hell did we decide we weren’t allowed to take things any further? That we had to remain platonic friends?”

Rebecca shrugged. “I think it was just an unwritten rule, neither of us wanting to ruin what we had. I felt the same.” She was numb just having this conversation, knowing that if she’d only said something, if they’d only…*it isn’t worth thinking about the past like that.* Her heart didn’t need to be damaged any more than it already was.

“I say to hell with rules, then.” Ben’s voice was softer now, but it packed an even greater punch than before. “Whenever you want to take things further, how about you just tell me this time around, huh?”

She cleared her throat. “I can’t deal with complications, Ben, which is why I’ve kind of avoided getting involved with anyone.” It was a lie—she hadn’t let anyone close because no one had ever measured up to him, and because she didn't want to introduce Lexie to a man.

"How about we take this one day at a time and don't put any labels on what we are?" he asked. "We're friends, nothing's going to change that, but if you want more, well, then, what'd be wrong with that?"

Rebecca opened her mouth to reply, needing to set the record straight and say something, when her phone sounded out, its shrill ring almost sending her off her chair.

"Shivers!" she gasped, grabbing it and pushing a side button to mute the loud volume.

Ben picked up his fork and started to eat again, as if they'd been having a conversation about food instead of sex.

"Oh, it's home," she said by way of explanation, reading the screen. "Sorry, I'll have to take it."

Rebecca put her hand over her mouth and spoke quietly into the mouthpiece.

"Hey, Mom. Don't tell me, she's trying to convince you to give her ice cream in bed?" She laughed into the phone but her smile faded when she was greeted with a big sob.

"Bec, oh, I…" Her mom sobbed down the line at her. "We're at the hospital."

Rebecca felt an ice-cold shiver pierce her spine. This could not be happening. *The hospital?*

"Slow down. Talk me through it. Tell me what's happened."

Ben dropped his fork to his plate, worried eyes meeting hers. She shook her head and reached for her purse.

"I thought she was just coming down with a cold, but then her temperature spiked. About an hour after going to bed she went all floppy and the alarm went off on the thermometer and…" Her mom sobbed again. "I'm so sorry to bother you, Bec, when you're finally taking some time to yourself."

Rebecca was trying to keep her voice calm but tears had welled in her eyes like huge stones, her voice choking at the thought of something happening to her little girl. "Is she okay now?" She stood and indicated to Ben with a nod of her head toward the door that they had to go. He jumped up straight away, throwing his napkin down and pulling out his wallet.

"She's doing fine, but she's asking for you."

"I'm coming now," she said, sounding more confident than she was. If there was one thing she'd always been good at it was staying calm in an emergency. "Just tell her I love her and that I'll be there soon."

She watched as Ben quickly paid the bill, racing back to her and walking with her to the door. When she hung up, she took a big, shuddering breath and pushed her phone into her pocket. Tears filled her eyes, burned like fire as she thought about Lexie without her.

"Bec?"

She glanced across at Ben, let him take her hand when he reached for it, linking their fingers. "It's Lexie," she managed, her breath coming in short pants as she tried to stay calm. She needed to tell him now but the words were choking her.

"Whatever it is, she'll be fine, okay?" Ben reassured, forcing her to stop and holding her hand tight as he looked down at her. "I'll drive you wherever we need to go, and we'll get there fast. So don't worry." His eyes were determined, strong, sexy all rolled into one.

"Thanks," Rebecca muttered, keeping hold of his hand. Her heart was hammering, mouth dry as she tried to swallow. All she cared about was getting to Lexie, but if Ben insisted on coming into the hospital with her? Then tonight was going to get a whole lot tougher than it already was.

He ran ahead of her when they were close to the car, unlocking it and flinging open her door before running around to the other side. She jumped in and fixed her seat belt.

"I know she'll be okay but…" Rebecca took a deep breath. "What if it's something more serious? What if it's…?"

"Let's just take this one step at a time, okay?"

Rebecca nodded and sunk as deep into the seat as she could, wishing she'd just stayed home. Wishing she'd never said yes to seeing Ben, wishing she'd just come straight out and told him the day he'd walked into her restaurant.

"We'll be there in less than an hour, Bec. Just hold tight and we'll be there before you know it."

"I'm sorry about dinner," she murmured, wondering how things had gone from seeming so perfect to being so, so awful in such a short time.

"Dinner? Are you kidding me?" Ben made a sort of grunting sound. "You have nothing to apologize for. This is your little girl we're talking about."

The car traveled fast, gravel spitting out behind them as they left the small side road and hit the main highway back to Melbourne city. Once they were cruising fast, the road dark except for a handful of cars up ahead or passing them, he reached for her, his hand clasping hers again and settling on her thigh.

Ben glanced at her, but she couldn't look back. Tears stung her eyes again, a pain in her chest that she'd only ever felt before when she'd waved Ben goodbye at the airport and believed she'd never see him again.

"Hey," he said softly.

She took a deep, shuddering breath, then angled her body slightly so she could see his face.

"Everything's going to be just fine, Bec. I promise."

She braved a smile, but she didn't believe him for a second. He had no idea whether everything was going to be okay or not. And even worse than that? She knew, in her heart, that she'd never stopped loving him. Not for a second. Only before, she'd imagined that when he did come home one day, he'd have a glamorous wife on his arm; a wife who was happy not having children, who just wanted to be the fun-loving, polo-wife party girl. In that scenario she believed they'd never have even had a chance to rekindle what they might have had. *Never* in a million years had she thought he'd come home single.

Instead, Ben had come back the same rugged, down-to-earth guy she'd always loved. Single, strong and even more handsome than ever. And so instead of resenting him or knowing she'd been right in not telling him what had happened after their night together, she was thinking all sorts of dangerous what-ifs. And those kinds of thoughts were capable of breaking a girl's heart, if the slow, painful shattering of hers was anything to go by.

And it wasn't *her* little girl she was worried about. *It was theirs.*

CHAPTER EIGHT

BEN FELT UTTERLY HELPLESS. He had no idea how to comfort Bec, didn't even know where to start, but what he could do was drive fast and get her into the hospital before her little girl had a chance to get really upset about her mom not being there. He slowed to turn into the hospital, gripping the steering wheel tight beneath his fingers.

"We're here," he said, scanning for the nearest park and pulling into the space.

He looked across at Bec; she was white as a sheet and her hands were trembling.

"Come on, I'll take you in." He hadn't planned on going in with her, thought she'd rather just be with her family, but she looked like she needed some help.

It was as though she'd been jolted from a dream then, lurching into action and pushing her door open, eyes suddenly flashing as she glanced over at him.

"You don't have to come," she said as she hurried toward the front entrance, breaking into a jog. "I'll be fine."

He grunted, catching up to her. "I'll get you to your daughter and then go." Ben didn't say anything, but just in case they were somehow at the wrong place or they'd already gone home, he wanted to be able to drive her.

Bec reached for him and he took her hand, both of them hurrying through the entrance.

"Thanks," she said as they waited at the elevator, her eyes meeting his.

"Bec, I'd never leave you when you needed me. It's no problem."

She gulped and took her hand back, folding them tight across her chest. He frowned as he watched her fidget, wondering if he'd somehow said the wrong thing. But that was being stupid. She was a mom scared about the health of her daughter; now was not the time to go reading into her body language.

They stepped into the elevator and headed to the right floor, with Bec checking her phone for the hundredth time to reread the text from her mom.

"We're here," Ben said as the doors opened and they rushed out. "I'll go find out where to…"

"Lexie!" Bec's high-pitched call echoed straight through his ear. "Lexie!"

Bec pushed past him, running fast in her heels and then dropping to her knees and throwing her arms around a little girl. Her hair was dark brown with streaks of blond through it, her arms wrapped tight around her mom's neck.

Ben stood back, not needing to be part of it. And then Bec's mom saw him and a smile broke out on her face, the worried frown lines disappearing when she locked eyes with him. He slowly made his way over, opened his arms and gave her a warm hug.

"Ben! What a lovely surprise."

He kissed her cheek before letting her go. "Sorry I stole your daughter away for the evening."

She pursed her lips. “Rebecca? Don’t be silly. That girl needed some time to herself. Between the restaurant and her little one, she doesn’t exactly take any time off.”

“Her daughter?” Ben asked.

“Is going to be fine. The doctor said there’s some nasty viruses going around, probably something she picked up in preschool. They said she was better off going home and having a good sleep in her own bed now that her fever has broken. The worst has long passed.”

Bec stood up then, her daughter in her arms. “Ben, you can’t drive all the way back to Geelong again tonight.”

He laughed. “It’s only an hour. I’ll be fine.”

“Stay with Rebecca,” her mom said, patting his shoulder before moving toward her daughter and kissing her granddaughter. “Granddad’s gone to bring the car around front. Why don’t you meet us at Rebecca’s?”

Ben looked at Bec, didn’t want to do anything that would make her uncomfortable, but all she seemed worried about was her daughter.

"Are you sure?" he asked, eyes never leaving Bec's.

"You drove me all this way and we ran out on dinner. Having you back to my place is the least I can do."

"Well that's settled, then," her mom said, looking pleased with herself and striding off ahead of them.

"If we just change Lexie's seat into your car, we can go straight to my place and let my folks go home."

He nodded and followed. It should have been awkward tagging along with her family, but they'd been part of each other's lives for so many years that it just didn't. He blew out a sigh of relief as the elevator dinged and they all stepped in, watching Bec with her girl tucked tight into her arms. It was a dose of reality seeing her in mom mode, told him that he had to tread carefully, but it didn't scare him. Not yet. Because he wanted Rebecca. *He needed Rebecca.* And he doubted anything was going to change that, little girl or not.

* * *

Rebecca shut the door and padded quietly back to the lounge. Ben was sitting back on the sofa, eyes shut, and she hoped he wasn't actually asleep.

"Ben?" she whispered once she was standing in front of him.

His eyes popped open, a slow smile breaking out on his face when he saw her.

"Hey. Is she asleep?"

"Snoring her little head off already," Rebecca said. "I was going to snuggle her up in my bed, but she went happily into her own. Her temperature's fine and she seemed happy enough."

He nodded, his eyes on hers. She took a deep breath, staring at him, wishing she could just ignore the way she felt for him and carry on like she had been these past few years. But she couldn't. The one man she'd ever loved was sitting on her sofa, looking back at her, and there was no way she could resist him, even if it was under false pretenses.

Rebecca moved fast, not wanting to give herself time to doubt; one moment she was standing in front of him, the next she was straddling him, her thighs on either side of his.

Ben didn't question, he just went with it, hands on her hips as she dipped her head and kissed him, lips over his, tasting him, doing what she'd only dreamed about doing for so long. His mouth was warm against hers, his hands skimming up her body, fingers tangling in her hair.

She pushed back for a second, trying to catch her breath, wondering what the hell she was doing. She'd resisted him for so many years, always determined never to be the one to make the first move, but after the night they'd just had…

"You okay?" Ben asked, one hand stroking her face as he gazed up at her.

"You said to tell you if I wanted this," she murmured, moistening her dry lips with her tongue.

He chuckled. "I did."

"Well, this is what I want," she said, refusing to give in to her insecurities. "Just tonight. Just once."

He nodded, his palm cupped to her cheek as he

guided her back forward. "Your wish," he muttered, "is my command."

Rebecca relaxed into his touch, sighed into his mouth as he kissed her so gently, his lips soft to start with, then rougher, more insistent as his hands explored under her top, skimming across her skin. Her body hummed, every part of her on edge, reactive to his fingertips, to his mouth, to *anything* he did to her. She should have made him a bed on the sofa and gone to her own room alone, but she couldn't. Because she needed Ben like she'd never needed anything in her life before.

She worked the buttons of his shirt, undoing them slowly one by one, moaning as he took his lips off hers and started plucking gentle kisses down her neck, inching toward her collarbone. There was an urgency to his touch, to the way she was touching him, just like their first and only ever night together.

Just one night. She just needed one night with Ben. No questions, no thinking about the past. Just one selfish night of being with him.

She could worry about the rest in the morning.

* * *

Ben cradled Bec in his arms, wishing he could just carry her to her room and keep her tight against him for the rest of the evening. But they weren't just two single people anymore; she had a daughter to worry about, which meant he couldn't exactly be naked in her bed come morning.

"I don't want you to think I'm running out on you, because I'd like nothing better than to spend the next twenty-four hours exploring every inch of you, but I think I'll head home."

Her eyes popped open. She'd been curled against him like a cat who couldn't get enough of being petted, and now she was pushed back and staring at him.

"You want to go already?"

He dropped a kiss to lips plump from all the attention his mouth had been giving them. "I don't want to, but it might be easier. You know, with Lexie."

She sighed and dropped her head to his chest again. "You're right. You're absolutely right."

"You going to the polo next weekend?" he asked.

Rebecca nodded against him. "Half for fun, half for work. I need to oversee catering to one of the corporate areas."

He stroked her hair, the golden blond strands like silk against his fingers. "It'll be the first time I've ever gone for fun, although I have offered to play if they need me."

She ran her hand down his arm. "We never missed a year, did we?"

"No, we didn't." He tucked his fingers under her chin, tilted her face up to him so he could kiss her again and look into her blue eyes. "So I'll see you on Saturday?"

She nodded. "Yes."

"It's a date, then."

Rebecca shook her head. "This was a one-time thing, Ben."

"So says you," he joked straight back.

"I'm serious. We can't do this again."

He laughed at her solemn expression. "We'll see."

She stayed silent, but she didn't pull away until a noise down the hall sent her scrambling for her clothes.

"I think that's my cue," he said.

Rebecca paused and bent down, her lips seeking out his in one long, slow kiss. "Drive safely."

He watched as she hurried toward her daughter's room, waiting until she'd disappeared from sight before reaching for his jeans. Their lives had changed, hell, everything had changed, but now that he'd had her once, he wasn't going to give her up again without a fight.

CHAPTER NINE

THE CROWD WAS BUZZING. Women dressed in tiny dresses and super-high heels were drinking champagne, most of them completely ignoring what was happening on the field, their male counterparts swilling imported beer and looking more interested in the horses galloping past toward the goalposts. It was amazing being part of the event here, but she could only imagine what it was like in the exclusive areas of the Argentinian or London polo scenes.

Bec wiggled her toes, wishing she hadn't worn brand-new shoes. They were bright yellow stilettos and they looked fabulous, but her feet were protesting big-time.

"Hey, gorgeous."

A shiver ran through her body. Suddenly her feet were the least of her worries. Rebecca slowly turned, recognizing Ben's deep, sexy voice. She'd avoided his calls during the week, not wanting to talk about their night together because then she'd have to feel guilty all over again. But she'd known he'd find her today; the only question had been when.

"Hey," she said, his gaze filled with enough heat to set her on fire.

"You enjoying the game?"

Bec laughed. "Probably more than you are. I bet you'd rather be playing than watching."

He shrugged. "Hey, what's one year watching? I'll be back on the team before I know it."

"Confident, much?" she said with a laugh.

He took a step closer to her and her resolve died. So much for telling him that she couldn't be anything more than friends with him, for swallowing her fears and breaking the news to him that she'd kept something from him and couldn't go on not telling him the truth today.

"Are you all done with work?" he asked, brushing back one of her curls that had separated from the others.

She swallowed, stuck in the web of his gaze. "Almost."

"You look beautiful today," he said, looking her up and down, his smile taking her breath away.

Rebecca stayed silent. She'd be lying if she said she hadn't made a massive effort on her appearance because she'd known he was going to be there, because she knew she'd end up spending time with him. She'd brought a new dress and heels to wear, showing off more skin than she ever usually would, her hair set in soft curls that made her feel all '50s pinup with her bright red lipstick.

"We have plenty of food if you're hungry and…"

Ben laughed and reached for her hand. "In case you haven't noticed I've been trying to get hold of you this week. It's not your food that I'm interested in."

Rebecca wanted to flirt with him, to let him tug her toward the polo field so they could watch the final chukker, hear more about his time away and what it was like, so they could reminisce and have fun. But she couldn't lie to him any longer, the weight of what she'd kept from him burning into her conscience.

"Ben, we need to talk."

He laughed, linking his fingers with hers. "How about we talk later and play now."

It broke her heart to see him like this. This was the old Ben, the Ben she'd had fun with all her life, the Ben she'd always remembered. She wanted to keep this version of him committed to memory, because when he heard what she had to say…

Ben frowned. "Okay, come on. Let's go sit by the field and you can tell me whatever's worrying you so much."

She grabbed a glass of champagne from a passing waiter, taking a few sips to calm her nerves. Ben kept hold of her other hand and she followed him through the crowd, wishing they were just two people having fun, that she could let her hair down and pretend like nothing had changed between them. But she'd already done that. Now it was time for the truth.

* * *

"So what is it that you're so desperate to tell me?" he asked, sitting down beside Bec and facing the field. He was reluctant to admit it but he was kind of enjoying being on the sidelines, for one day anyway. His granddad was out there somewhere, close to the action, watching horses he'd trained and sold thunder around the field, and Ben was just happy to be back at the famous Melbourne Polo in the City.

"Ben, I don't think there's an easy way to tell you this, so I'm just going to come out and say it."

He frowned. The expression on her face had him worried, her eyes filled with what looked to be…tears? What the hell was she upset about?

"Bec, what's wrong?"

"You're her father, Ben. I know I should have told you sooner, that I shouldn't have kept it from you, but Lexie's your daughter."

Ben froze. No part of his body moved, not so much as a quiver as he stared at her. The smile had long disappeared from Bec's mouth, and now his did, too.

"*What*?" He must have misheard her. She'd said he was…

"I know it's probably hard for you to make sense of right now, but Lexie's your daughter. I just couldn't…"

"Hold on a minute." He pushed back his chair, needing to put distance between them, to just stare at Rebecca for a moment and try to figure out what the hell she was trying to explain to him. "You're saying that our one night together, that I…" Ben jumped up, running his hand hard through his hair and grinding his teeth together. "I'm her *father*?"

He turned back to Rebecca to see tears sliding down her cheeks. She wasn't making a noise, silently crying.

"I'm sorry."

"Damn right you should be sorry!" he hissed. "I've been back here all this time, we've been with each other, and you never thought this should be the first thing you tell me?" His head was pounding, fury building inside him. "You had no right to keep this from me."

She nodded but he didn't care how upset she was. He'd come back desperate to see her again, to spend time with the one and only woman he'd ever trusted, and she'd blindsided him with this. How the hell could he be a father? He'd thought she was different, that after all the fake women more interested in fame and money he'd been surrounded with, that Bec was different. That he'd never have to worry about her not being honest. And now—he swallowed. Hard.

"Ben, I..."

"Mommy!"

The high-pitched voice calling out shattered every thought in his mind. He turned slowly, seeing a blond-haired little girl running fast, arms pumping as she made her way toward Rebecca. She flew into her mother's arms as he just stared on, watching in disbelief.

"She was so excited about coming." Ben stayed still as he listened to Rebecca's mother calling out. "Is she okay with you now?"

"Yes, she's fine," Rebecca called back.

Ben couldn't take his eyes off the girl. *Off his*

daughter. All this time he'd been furious that some jerk had left Rebecca to be a solo parent, without ever guessing that that someone could have been him. And now that he looked at her… every part of him ached, with anger or resentment or disbelief; he had no idea which.

And now that she was here, he had to suck up every bit of anger that he wanted to hurl at Rebecca and save it for later. Because he wouldn't lose his temper in front of a child, and he sure as hell wouldn't do it in front of *his* child.

It was time for them to leave, and he wasn't going to let Rebecca get away without explaining everything to him. He wanted answers now and he wasn't taking no for an answer.

CHAPTER TEN

"WE'RE GOING BACK to Geelong." His words were meant as a statement, not a question. He stood staring at her, his height advantage suddenly daunting as he stood too close. "And Lexie's coming with us."

Rebecca stood her ground, refusing to be intimidated. She might have done the wrong thing in lying to him all this time, but she'd done it to protect her daughter and she'd do anything to keep her protected and in her safe little cocoon forever if she had to. She folded her arms across her chest, not giving in to the tremor of fear running through her body.

"I think we're best to just head back to my place."

Ben smiled at Lexie, touching her shoulder before moving to stand closer to Rebecca, his eyes burning into her with none of the kindness in his gaze that he'd just shown Lexie.

"We've got a lot to talk about, Rebecca," he said. "We'll go by your place and get Lexie's things, then we're heading to Geelong."

"You need to understand why I…"

"Enough," he said, his voice so low it was only just audible. "There's nothing you can say right now, Rebecca, so just don't."

When Ben finally turned away she let out a big breath she hadn't even realized she was holding. He bent to say something to Lexie, made her smile, then walked off. His long legs ate up the ground as she watched him, at the same time as she almost collapsed from fear.

"Mommy?"

Lexie's little voice was like an injection of energy to her body. She picked herself up and fixed a smile, bending down and holding out an arm to her.

"We're going on an adventure tonight. What do you think about going to visit Ben's farm?"

"Yay!"

Rebecca scooped her up and waved goodbye to her staff as she passed by where they were still working. They were almost done packing up and there was nothing left for her to do, and besides, there was no point in delaying the inevitable.

"Can we go now?"

Rebecca nodded and pressed a kiss to Lexie's forehead. "We sure can."

A fresh wave of fear washed through her, but she forced it away. There was no point in fearing the unknown. Trouble was, when it involved her little girl's future, it was impossible not to worry.

Rebecca turned and looked back at her daughter. She'd fallen asleep. They weren't even ten minutes out of the city and she had already succumbed to slumber. Her get out of jail free card was snoozing, which meant the interrogation was just about to start.

"She's asleep," she said, moving back to her sitting position as far away from Ben as possible. If she could have put a bigger gap between them in the car then she would have—in fact she'd prefer him on a plane heading back to Argentina if she had a choice right now. It might be her car they were driving in, but it felt like she was a prisoner.

He didn't answer. Rebecca glanced over and saw the tight clench of his jaw. She wasn't looking forward to this at all.

"What were you even thinking keeping this from me?" he demanded, his voice low. "You've had every opportunity to tell me, Rebecca."

She sighed and looked out the window. At the buildings blurring past, the inky-black sky, other cars whizzing by. All this time she'd wondered how it would happen. Whether Lexie would be a child or an adult, and now here she was, about to explain why she'd kept a secret that was going to ruin their friendship forever.

"Well?"

He clearly wasn't going to let her get away with staying silent, not now that Lexie was asleep.

"I don't know where to begin," she said honestly, her thoughts a jumble.

"How about starting with the part where you

forgot to tell me I was a father." His voice was like ice, so cold he could have turned her to stone.

Rebecca knew he had every right to hate her, to be angry with her, but the steel-edged ring to his tone scared her. She had acted how she thought best at the time. Yes, it was flawed, but if it were to happen all over again, she'd probably do the same. She hadn't done it to hurt him, she'd done it because she cared enough about him to let him go.

"I found out when I was two months pregnant," she started, digging her fingernails deep into her palm to force pain other than what she was feeling in her heart. It had hurt at the time; the hurt had been so bad she'd been curled into a ball on the floor, cradling her belly, wishing she could make everything right and go back in time, her tears a puddle on the bathroom tiles beneath her. But this pain was stabbing, relentlessly washing over her in thick waves. She'd been so broken, so damaged already over everything, and then there had been Lexie. And from the day she'd been born, everything had changed; she'd had someone to love and pour all her energy into, and she'd never wished her baby away or resented her for a moment.

There was silence as she waited for Ben to do the math. She knew he would.

"So when I came home for that week, before I flew back for my first pro game in Europe, you knew then?"

His voice was incredulous and she swallowed down tears. A show of emotion now would only make her look pathetic, and it was Ben who should be upset and angry, not her. This was his time to be hurt, not hers.

"I'd just found out. When you came home I was so pleased to see you but, damn it, Ben! You had your whole future planned and there was no way I was going to ruin your life, to clip your wings and hold you back. I wasn't going to let history repeat itself."

"Don't..." He lowered his voice. "Don't give me that. I had a right to know. You can't put this on me when I never had the chance to be a part of our child's life, when you never let it be my choice."

She took a deep, slow breath. "What's the one thing you've always told me? The one thing you were always so sure about your future?"

Rebecca could see how tight his grip on the steering wheel was, his body rigid as he glowered at the road. "Don't you turn this around on me, don't you dare."

"You said you never wanted to be a dad," she continued, undeterred. Now she'd started she couldn't stop. "You said you never wanted to be a parent because of your mom, because of what she did to you. That you never wanted to have a child and ever let them think they'd held you back from doing what you wanted to do with your life." She shook her head and turned to stare at him. "Tell me I'm wrong, Ben. Tell me I'm not saying the exact words you said to me so many times, that that wouldn't have been exactly what would have happened."

He was silent. The only noise was the tires on

the road and it only made her mouth dryer, the pounding in her head louder.

"Ben..."

"Don't you dare put words in my mouth," he growled out, slamming one palm against the steering wheel. "Whatever the hell I said had nothing to do with *our kid.* Hell, Bec, I know what it was like to grow up without my parents. I would never do that to a child, to our..." His voice trailed off, as if he had no idea what to say next.

"I didn't even know if I was going to go through with it when you were back," she said in a low voice. "I was alone, I knew my family would be devastated, and I just needed the time to get my head around it all. To deal with...*me.*"

Ben looked over at her. "What changed your mind?"

"You." She said the word simply, without hesitation.

"Me?" His focus was entirely back on the road now, but his laugh was low and cynical. "You kept it from me, but somehow *I* helped to change your mind."

"I loved you, Ben. I couldn't terminate what we'd made." She quickly brushed stray tears away as they trickled down her cheek. "You have to believe me, that I wanted to do right by you, that I would never have kept it from you if I hadn't known you would resent me or her. Because I know you, I knew you better than you probably even knew yourself back then, and that meant I knew you'd stay with me, *with us*, out of duty."

He didn't respond and she squirmed, wishing she could get out of the car. It was starting to feel very claustrophobic and if she didn't have Lexie curled up in the backseat she'd have demanded he stop the car and let her the hell out.

"I didn't want to hold you back. I knew you'd feel obliged to do the honorable thing, and I didn't want to stand in the way of your future." She bit back a sob. "Look at your mom, what that did to you knowing that she'd compromised her medical career to have you. You forget that I was there for you when you tried to reconnect with her, that I saw how much she hurt you. I didn't want you to end up making the same mistakes as she did, when you didn't even have a choice in the matter."

"I still had a right to know." He punched out each word. "No matter what you thought or what I'd said or what we'd been through, I still had a right to know."

"I know you did," she whispered. "I know."

Rebecca felt dreadful, but she deserved it.

"I'm sorry, Ben, but I did what seemed best at the time," she said, needing him to at least understand why she'd done what she'd done. "It may have been the wrong decision, but I was young, scared and alone."

"I would have been there for you, Bec," he responded, his voice back to his soft, understated tone. "I would have stood by you. *Damn it*! You know I would have."

She let out a heaving breath.

"And that's exactly why I didn't tell you."

Lexie moaned in her sleep as Ben pulled her up into his arms. It was the first time they'd touched, other than when he'd dropped his hand to her shoulder earlier in the day. Shadows played across the girl's face as he carried her up to the house, and Ben watched each one. The way the light fell over his daughter's skin did something to him, hurt him somehow, and it took all his strength not to pass her to Rebecca. The last thing he wanted was to hold her, to be close to her when…hell, he didn't even know what to think.

He could hear Rebecca following behind, but he didn't acknowledge her. She could follow them upstairs, and when they got to the guest room she could take over. As much as he wanted to not be close to Lexie, something else was making him want to keep her close forever, to know what it was like to hold a child that was his own flesh and blood.

"She can sleep in bed with me," Rebecca whispered to him.

Ben nodded and kept walking. Lexie stirred but didn't wake, and Ben waited until Rebecca had rearranged the bedding before placing her on the mattress. He pulled the sheet and covers up under her chin and watched her long and hard before turning away. Rebecca was staring at him but he went straight past her and back downstairs.

Only hours ago, he'd been ready to ask Rebecca for something more, to apologize for leaving her behind in the first place and ask if they could be something more. If he was honest with himself he knew something had been wrong, that there had been more going on than her simply not wanting to leave her family, but he'd been desperate to get away and he'd decided not to ask questions. It had been Argentina, playing polo for one of the best teams in the world, or staying home and hoping that the girl who'd been his best friend for years might want something more. By the time they'd spent the night together, he'd already signed on the dotted line and cashed his first check from the team, and his flight was booked to go. It had been too late to change his mind even if he'd wanted to.

He was so angry with her his blood was boiling, but as much as he wanted to hate her and put all the blame on her, it wasn't all her fault. Maybe he was just tired, shell-shocked, but he could barely wrap his head around the whole situation. *A daughter.* She looked like him—her eyes were the same deep shade of brown, beautiful against golden hair the same color as her mom's. And from the desperation, the anguish he'd seen on Rebecca's face earlier, he knew there was no point in asking if she was sure about the girl's paternity. She was his; as true as the fact the sun would rise every morning, Lexie was his daughter.

Ben tripped his way down the stairs, his brain on the verge of exploding. Just when he'd thought life was going to get simpler, that things were going to be easy back home and he might have a chance of connecting with the woman he'd left behind, he was faced with this. With a daughter. A child of his own when he'd never even considered the fact that he might be a father in his lifetime, when he'd just gotten his head around the idea of being a fun kind of uncle to the girl if he and Bec did finally become more permanently involved.

A noise upstairs told him that Rebecca was on

her way down, which meant this was all about to become very real, very fast. He stifled the bellow he felt like roaring and reasoned with himself that a drink was what he needed. A very, very strong one. Or two. *Or three.*

Rebecca found Ben sitting at the kitchen table. He had a tumbler in front of him and she watched as he took a sharp swig of the golden brown liquid as she walked into the room. Unless he'd changed his habits since leaving, Rebecca knew that Ben wasn't much of a drinker. He'd always liked the odd beer, but definitely not spirits and certainly not straight. It made her eyes water just looking at straight whiskey.

"Want one?" Ben asked, raising his eyes.

She nodded. Rebecca had never drunk straight spirits before, not once, but she didn't think that now was the right time to say no.

Ben downed what was left in his tumbler before going into the kitchen, dropping a few ice cubes into his glass and into a fresh one, then pouring a small portion of whiskey into each.

"Jack Daniel's on the rocks," he announced, his glare still cold as ice.

She took a tiny sip and felt her eyes well with tears as she swallowed. Her throat was on fire as the liquid traced a fiery path right to her belly, then ignited all over again.

"It gets better," he said, downing another quick gulp. "Just keep drinking."

Rebecca didn't recall ever feeling quite this awkward, and especially not with the one person in the world she'd always been able to be herself around. She took another hesitant sip. It still tasted awful but not as bad as the first, and if it helped her feel a bit less anxious about the whole situation, then maybe it would be worth it.

"So where to from here?" Ben asked. "What the hell are we going to do?"

He was staring at her, which was worse than just seeing his angry side profile in the car, although maybe the alcohol was starting to numb her system a little because he didn't seem quite as irate.

"I know you hate me for what I've done," she

said. "But I am sorry, Ben, more sorry than you'll ever understand. And I need you to get that I didn't do this to hurt you. The last few years have been rough, but no matter how tough it got I didn't want to be the one to shatter your dreams. Then as time passed, I didn't want it to be Lexie you resented." She shrugged. "*Me*, sure, but the idea that you could blame my gorgeous little girl?"

"*Our*," he corrected. "*Our* gorgeous little girl, Bec. The fact that she's ours is why it wasn't your secret to keep. Why you should have let me decide if I wanted to come home for her, if she was more important to me than my career."

"I'm sorry. There's nothing more I can say." Rebecca wrapped one arm tight around herself. "I'm sorry a thousand times over, Ben, and I need you to believe me." She bit her lip hard to stop the tears from falling.

"What if I'd not come back for another few years, though? What if we'd never bumped into one another? Would you have ever told me? Would I still be walking around not knowing that I had a beautiful little girl out there in the world?"

Rebecca realized there was no point in lying, because she wasn't going to hold back now that Ben knew. "No. I wouldn't have sought you out to tell you, if that's what you're asking. Not if you hadn't come home of your own free will."

He glared at her and took another long sip of his drink, draining the glass.

"Just because you're her mom doesn't mean you have a right to keep your daughter's father from her," Ben snapped. "I could understand a mother protecting her child from a violent person, from a drug addict, from some lowlife they're better off not knowing. But hell, Rebecca, did you really think I'd be *that bad* a parent? That I couldn't man the hell up and deal with the consequences of what had happened between us, of what we'd made?"

"No!" she almost yelled the word. "I wanted you to live the life you wanted to live, not come back here for me. For a baby you didn't choose to have." She bit back a sob, a torrent of emotion that choked her. "Don't you see, Ben? I know what a great dad you'd be, but you didn't want a child. You wanted to travel the world playing polo with the best players in the world, and that's exactly what I wanted you to do."

"I would have, though," he said, his stare unrelenting. "I would have dropped everything to look after you. I would have stayed." Ben shook his head. "Or I would have taken you with me. Either way I wouldn't have just left you. If you'd even just told me how you felt about me, not insisted that you wanted us to just be friends, this all could have changed."

"If you came home for me, I wanted it to be because you loved me, wanted me, not because you felt obliged to." She forced a smile. "I have always wanted a family, Ben, you've always known that. There was no way I could ever see us working long term because we wanted different things, which is why I wanted to stay friends. And that was before I knew I was pregnant. Loving you wasn't enough."

"But *I did love you.*"

He said the words so softly, so honestly that it was like a sucker punch straight to her stomach. He was lying, he was… She bit back a sob, shaking her head as she balled her fists. She'd waited so long to hear those words, and now she had, it was too late. Because he already hated her. Because she'd already ruined everything. But it still didn't change the fact that they'd always wanted different things.

"But was I wrong? Did you want the same as me?"

"No." He shook his head. "I loved you because you were you, because I thought you would never lie to me, never betray me." He shook his head. "I thought I knew you."

"Ben, please don't…" His words were like a knife piercing her skin, the pain so intense she could hardly stand it.

Ben watched her long and hard before standing. "If you'd been honest with me, everything would have been different. *Everything.*"

He walked his now-empty glass back into the kitchen and slammed his hand down hard on the counter, his fury so fierce her hands started to tremble just watching him. She stayed silent, watching, listening, waiting. Ben didn't talk until he returned to the room, his eyes finally meeting hers, the storm in his gaze like a cyclone. She watched as he leaned against the wall, his big frame rigid with tension. She saw her daughter in him as she studied his face, in the line of his mouth and the slant of his eyes. That was how Lexie looked when she was cross with her, when Rebecca didn't give her what she wanted. Only Lexie's minor temper tantrums had nothing on the fierce stare and angry-bear hulk facing her now who looked as though he was capable of crushing anything in his path with his bare hands.

"Do your parents know?" His voice was low and husky, so deep it tugged every single one of her heartstrings.

She swallowed and dipped her head. "Nobody knows. Just me."

He raised his eyebrows in question. She knew

she'd just sunk even lower in his opinion than she already had.

"I told them that I had a one-night stand, that it was some jerk I never saw again." She paused and looked up at him before going back to picking at her nails. "They had no reason not to believe me, aside from the fact that I've always been Ms. Responsible. The difficult part would have been believing I'd actually had random sex, not the fact the guy had bailed."

"And you're telling me no one ever put two and two together?" His glare was cool again, his entire face frosty.

"I guess you see what you want to see. You'd been gone a long time before she started to look like you, and thankfully no one ever made the connection." She sighed. "It's one of the reasons I never came to see Gus again, because I didn't want to lie to his face. And besides, no one knew about what happened between us, did they? As far as everybody else was concerned we'd just parted as friends."

"What would have happened if I hadn't gone, Bec?"

"We would never have spent the night together," she said simply. "We would have stayed as friends, we wouldn't be having this conversation."

"You're sure about that?" he asked. "I never thought I was good enough for you, Bec. I knew that I couldn't give you what you wanted, but maybe we still would have ended up in bed together eventually."

"*You* not good enough for *me*?" She almost laughed. "That's the stupidest thing I've ever heard."

"I'm going to bed," he announced.

Rebecca merely nodded and stayed seated. She watched as he walked away. His shoulders were slumped, head down, hands jammed into his pockets. This wasn't the Ben McFarlane she knew. There was anger seething through his veins, she knew that, but she also guessed he was heartbroken. He would have thought he could always trust her, with the history they had behind them, and she knew he was probably as upset about her deception as he was about what she'd kept from him.

A painful tickle of concern played down her back, leaving her aching and worried. She could go and get Lexie and run, head back to her place since it was her car they'd brought, but that would only be delaying the inevitable. Besides, Ben would find them wherever they were. There had been a look in his eyes that said he was not going to be giving his girl up, and that frightened her more than anything.

"Ben!" she called out, jumping up and chasing after him.

He stopped, his hand on the bannister, about to walk up the stairs. He didn't say anything, but he didn't move, either.

"Ben, I want you to know that I loved you, too," she told him. "I loved you so bad it hurt, and if there was any way I thought we could have made it work, as a family, I'd have made that choice in a heartbeat."

He turned, slowly, his stormy gaze catching

hers as he stared, jaw locked hard. "Yeah? Well that ship has sailed, Bec. A long, long time ago."

She swallowed a wave of emotion, a tide of hurt and sadness exploding through her body. "Ben," she whispered. He turned and started to walk again, his back like a brick wall between them. "Ben!" she begged, louder this time, her voice full of unshed tears.

But he never turned back. She'd lost him. From the moment she'd told him, she'd lost him, and he'd just made his intentions very, very clear. It was over. Any little dreams she'd ever entertained about them reuniting, any fantasies she'd had about a perfect little family…that's all they were. Broken dreams and fantasies.

Ben was right. They were done.

There was no chance of finding sleep. Ben kept his eyes trained on the ceiling. Even in the dark he didn't feel tired. Exhausted in plenty of ways but not tired enough for sleep to seek him out. After the day he'd had he should be shattered, but he wasn't.

He was so angry with Rebecca the fury was consuming him; his body was on fire with a rage he'd never felt before. Which is why he'd walked away from her before he said something he'd regret forever. His grandfather had more patience than a handful of men put together, and he'd remembered that when he'd left Bec standing downstairs alone. He would have rather yelled at her, called her all sorts of names and slammed his fist through a wall; but he hadn't.

He had a daughter. *A daughter.* A little girl who was probably too young yet to have worried about not having a father, but he knew those thoughts would come soon. By the time he'd started school and seen all the other kids with both parents visiting on sports day and at science fairs, he'd realized he was the odd one out. Hardly any of the other kids had come from single parent homes back then. Add to that a mother who resented the time she'd had to spend with him, and he'd had a pretty lousy time when it came to parents. If it hadn't been for his granddad… He shook his head. He didn't even want to think about it. And now here he was, finding out that he was a dad, and no matter how furious he was with Rebecca, nothing changed the fact that he had a kid.

Ben lay another few moments, eyes shut, before getting up and pulling on his jeans, leaving his chest bare. He needed to talk to someone about this, someone other than Rebecca. Gus would be sound asleep by now, having left the game before them, but considering they might only have months left together, he doubted the old man would mind being woken. This affected both of them. Gus was now officially a great-grandfather, and Ben needed his advice. *Fast.*

There was a part of him that wanted to listen to Rebecca, that wanted to forgive her, but it just didn't seem possible. Not now. After all they'd gone through together, all the ups and downs over so many years, nothing changed the fact that she'd lied to him. Or omitted to tell him—no matter how he put it the fact didn't change. But he'd asked her about Lexie's father, that first time at the restaurant and then when they were out riding, which meant she'd had every opportunity to tell him.

He still would have been angry, hell, nothing could change how he felt, but to wait all this time?

There was nothing to like about what had happened, or how he'd found out, but he had to deal with the fact that he did have a daughter. That there were consequences to the night he and Rebecca had shared. The trouble was, he'd never have shut his own flesh and blood out of his life, never would have walked away. He'd never wanted to repeat his own mother's mistakes, and then he'd gone and done exactly that without even knowing.

He walked straight past the room Rebecca and Lexie were in and resisted the urge to push it open, not to seek Rebecca out, but to catch a glimpse of his daughter. When he looked at her, he knew he was a dad, could feel that the child who looked back was part of him. But the thought of living up to the title terrified him, just the idea of being around her or touching her, talking to her even, scaring him now that he knew he was her dad.

Ben gritted his teeth and kept moving, not stopping until he reached the other end of the long hall, tapping on his grandfather's door. He might not have had a dad growing up, but he'd had a darn good male role model. All this time he'd been scared of being a father because he didn't have his own to show him the ropes, hadn't had a parent to depend on, but he'd had Gus, and now that he was faced with being a dad to Lexie, he realized that he would know instinctively what to do, if he let himself. Because everything good in him, he'd learned from Gus. And no one could ever take that away from him.

CHAPTER ELEVEN

THERE WAS NO way to explain how she felt. Her entire body was aching, Lexie was jammed up hard against her, one arm slung over her face, and she was dead tired. Rebecca guessed that being caught out after years of hiding the truth wasn't meant to be easy, but she was exhausted. All night she'd writhed around on the sheets, trying not to disturb Lexie but desperately craving sleep—anything to give her some relief from reliving the conversations she'd had with Ben. He probably felt the same, racked with guilt and anger for different reasons. *And coming to terms with the fact that he had a daughter.*

Rebecca listened out but could hear no noise in the house. Both men had always been early risers, but given that it was Sunday she expected they might be a little later out of bed. Besides, she was desperate for a coffee to kick-start the morning. Running into Ben was a risk she'd have to take, and at the end of the day she was going to have to face him sometime. They were going to have to sort things out one way or another. To think that the last time they'd been together had been like heaven on earth, and now they were barely talking.

Once she'd pried herself out from her daughter's octopus-like grasp, she ran a quick brush through her hair, pulled it up into a ponytail and rummaged for a T-shirt. She looked down at her legs and left them bare—the T was superlong and she didn't have anything on show.

A quick glance back at Lexie reassured her she wasn't going to wake up while her mother was gone, and she slipped out the door, stopping in the hallway to listen out. She couldn't hear a thing. She tiptoed down the stairs, cringing when she hit a squeaky board and hurrying the rest of the way down. She padded across the timber floor to the kitchen, smiled when she inhaled the faint smell of coffee wafting around her. Gus must have made a pot last night; unless Ben had gotten back up from bed, she guessed the old man had been up, unable to sleep. Rebecca deposited the remains into the bin and scooped fresh granules from the container, just like old times. She'd always tried to be up first when she'd stayed over, making coffee and gulping down her first cup before Ben was awake, buzzed about training the polo ponies with him. By sunrise they'd always been galloping down the beach—Geelong was famous for being horse country, and the proximity to the beach for training was one of the reasons it was so popular.

The smell of fresh coffee made her smile. She could almost taste the strong flavor of black, sugary syrup just from inhaling it. A complete contradiction to her usually obsessive compulsive healthy, organic choice in whatever she put into her body, but it was a habit she'd never been able to break. No tea, herbal concoction, *nothing* could make her feel like coffee did, particularly in the morning.

She took a slow sip, inhaled the aroma and shut

her eyes for a second. With her eyes closed, she could be anywhere, drinking coffee at home, at the restaurant—hell, she could be at a resort in Fiji. Then she opened them, and looked straight out the window to the yellowed green grass fields beyond the house. But she wasn't *anywhere.* She was at the McFarlanes' place, she was with Ben, and she was guessing that at some stage today she was going to have to tell Lexie that she had a dad.

Ben stopped dead. He smelled the coffee, it had lulled him down from his bedroom, but he thought Gus had just got down before him like usual, when reality couldn't have been farther from the truth. Nothing could prepare him for what he found.

Rebecca had her back turned. She was fussing over what he presumed was the coffee press, and as far as he was concerned, she could do it all morning. He couldn't see much of her upper half, with the exception of the nape of her neck, which was exposed from her hair being pulled back. But her lower half. *Wow.* He'd never seen anything so sexy.

He hoped she had nothing on at all beyond that T-shirt, but he remembered she had always been fond of boy shorts. He'd hassled her about it for years, when she'd always laughed at other girls' obsessions with G-strings, but he guessed the boy shorts had become rather brief from what he could see of her bent forward. Because all he could see was an endless expanse of tanned, toned, slim legs, stretching up to what was an incredibly firm bottom. Hmm. It was starting to be a rather uncomfortable viewing experience.

Every single piece of him was furious with her still, even after talking to Gus late into the night, but the woman looked like something out of a men's magazine and he couldn't take his eyes off her.

Then she turned around. He didn't know what to do so he just stared back at her. The reality was, he wanted to shock her, take action instead of just standing there staring at her. He wanted to kiss the surprised pout straight off her lips.

Rip her shirt off to take his mind off the fact that she'd completely thrown him.

But hell, her front profile was even more tempting than the rear. She clearly had nothing on beneath the T-shirt, and it clung gently to her breasts. With her face free from makeup she looked more like the teenage Rebecca. Lips pillowy from sleep still, eyes slightly puffy, cheeks flushed.

"Morning." He wished he'd just turned and gone back to bed the minute he'd seen her down there.

She gave him a tight smile. Hardly the come-hither look his male organs were wishing for, even if he was angry with her.

"Hey," she replied.

"You're up early." He kept his distance as he moved into the kitchen and reached for a cup, not wanting to get anywhere close to her bare skin.

Rebecca shrugged. "Didn't get much sleep. But then I'm guessing you probably had a rough night, too."

Ben poured himself coffee and went straight

back out to the adjoining living room. He could still see her but it was far less arousing than being within a few feet of her. She even smelled amazing, which hadn't helped the fact that he was trying to ignore her.

They were both silent, sipping away soundlessly on their coffees, so much hanging between them that needed to be said. Had to be said. They shared a daughter, and that meant they had a lot to work out. No matter how he felt about her right now, they had to find a way to get past it enough to talk.

"Lexie's still asleep?"

Rebecca nodded. "She usually sleeps in a little after a late night."

Ben frowned and took another sip of his coffee. How the hell could they go from being strangers to friends again after so long, and then feel more like strangers than ever again, so fast? It made him furious and no matter how bad he wanted to be the better person here, he couldn't.

"Ben, I think we need—"

A noise stopped her midsentence and the same

noise made Ben put down his coffee. Lexie's little voice echoed out down the hall just before a blur rushed past Ben, hurtling at high speed toward Rebecca.

"Oh. Hey, honey." He watched as Bec scooped her up for a cuddle, but the little girl was wriggling again soon, running back in the same direction she'd come from and reappearing with Gus by her side. He had his cane in one hand and the other resting on Lexie's shoulder.

"Mommy, this is Gus."

Once they were both in the room she sidled back over to her mom, grinning at Gus as she held on to Rebecca's leg.

No, he's your great-granddad. Ben was on the verge of exploding, angry all over again, but one look at the sweet, innocent expression on the little girl's face pacified him.

"You okay, sweetie?" He listened to Rebecca talk to her, watched as she kissed her cheek. There was no mistaking they were mother and daughter, and the way Lexie gazed at her? It told him that no matter how much he hated what she'd done to him, what she'd kept from him, his daughter had been cared for by someone who adored her. There was no way a child could look at a mother like that unless she meant the world to her.

Lexie tucked her head against her mom's chest, peeking over at him. "I didn't know where you were."

Rebecca kissed her again before putting her to her feet. "I shouldn't have left you. Sorry, sweetheart."

"Then *he* found me," Lexie said, sticking her thumb out at Gus. "And he told me all about the horses he has. *Horses*, Mommy. *Horses*."

Ben stifled a smile. He guessed the old saying was true—the apple never did fall far from the tree.

"Gus does have some pretty special horses."

Rebecca looked up at Gus as she spoke. He was smiling, but he was also giving her a look. She could feel Ben behind her, still keeping his distance, but close enough to know that he was there. *Gus knew.* It was obvious from the way he was looking at them, and from the way he was going back and forth with his eyes from father to daughter as if he was putting two and two together. She forced a smile. It was tough to see them like this, to know that she'd caused so much hurt, especially if it meant losing the love and respect of two men who'd always meant so much to her.

"Lexie, Gus is Ben's granddaddy," she continued, trying to stop her voice from shaking. "Mr. McFarlane was very special to me when I was… younger."

Lexie smiled coyly at Gus.

"None of this Mr. McFarlane business," said Gus, swatting his hand through the air. Lexie giggled and put her head hard against Rebecca's chest. "We had a good old chat on the way downstairs, didn't we?"

Rebecca turned her body around so Lexie was facing Ben.

"You remember Ben from last night? Mommy's friend?"

"Yup," she said, smiling as Ben held his hand up in hello, his grin all for his daughter, his eyes lighting up in a way they'd used to do for her.

"Well, let's go get us changed shall we, miss? Then we can have some breakfast."

She carried Lexie back toward the stairs, the little girl still light enough to carry on her hip.

"Who's G-Gus?" Lexie got a bit stuck on the "G" sound and made Rebecca laugh.

"I told you," she said, pulling a T-shirt over her daughter's arms and harder over her head once they were in the bedroom. When she tugged it past her ears, she shook her head and grinned up at her. "He's Ben's granddad," she repeated, just in case she had actually forgotten, despite having told her twice already.

"Where's his dad?"

She suddenly didn't like the way this conversation was heading at all. Any conversation right now that involved daddy talk seemed dangerous.

"Ben's daddy? I'm not sure."

"What about my daddy? Why don't I have a daddy?"

Rebecca had walked straight into that one.

"Let's go back down for breakfast, huh?"

She had talked about her dad before. Or at least made up a father figure and stuck with the story. He was a very busy man and might never come home, all sorts of things, but as Lexie got older she had known it wasn't a question that could be so easily shirked, especially when she was trying to make sure her daughter felt loved even if she did have only one parent. And the lies no longer sounded convincing, not as she became older and understood so much more.

Lexie jumped up and grabbed her hand and Rebecca followed her out the door. She would have liked to spend some more time on her makeup but if this got her out of talking about daddies, then she was up for it.

"So, do you go to kindergarten or anything?"

Lexie nodded, a mischievous smile on her face. Ben was all out of ideas—there was only so much he could think to talk about with a three-year-old, but school seemed like a safe topic. He watched as his daughter munched on rice bubbles. Lucky Rebecca had thought to bring a stash, because they didn't have anything like that here.

He noticed Rebecca was taking a painstakingly long time to eat her toast. She was staring at the marmalade as if it was dangerous, not taking her eyes from it, nibbling delicately around the edges. Gus had gone out to do his rounds; hell, they were like some dysfunctional family, sitting together but not communicating.

"So I'm guessing you like horses," Ben said, refusing to give up on the conversation stakes just yet, even though he was as good as terrified just sitting here with her.

Lexie's reaction told him he'd finally hit the jackpot. Her eyes were wide, bright, and she slurped milk down her chin in her excitement.

"Have you ever ridden a horse?" Ben asked

"No." Phew, for a while there he'd wondered if he was ever going to come up with something they could talk about.

"You want to go for a ride with me today, then?"

"Like on a real horse?" Lexie had knocked her bowl forward and sent milk sloshing, but Ben couldn't have cared less. He finally felt like he was making some headway.

He chuckled. "Yeah, on a real horse. What do you say?"

"Let's go!"

"Ahem." Rebecca cleared her throat and smiled tightly at Ben. "Mommy needs to talk to Ben for a second, Lexie. You go and find your shoes."

Lexie sprinted off back toward the stairs and Ben glared at Rebecca.

"I'm not so sure about her riding," she said.

"She's coming riding with me today." Even if he had no idea how to talk to her or what to do, she was his and he needed to deal with it in his own way.

There was no chance he was negotiating on this. He'd gone all Lexie's life without making decisions, without having the chance to do things with her, and today that was going to change. He was a father, and that meant manning up and taking responsibility.

"Ben..." she protested again.

"No!" He thumped his mug down and pushed to his feet. "*No.* You had it your way, now it's my turn."

She cast her eyes down and Ben wished he hadn't spoken to her so harshly. He'd never spoken to her like that before and he didn't need to start now, no matter what had gone on between them. She was *Rebecca.* They had way too much history for him to be acting like a complete idiot. And besides, even though she'd lied to him, he still wanted her.. No matter how he'd like to pretend otherwise, his desire for Rebecca went beyond anything he was capable of controlling.

He wanted to hate her for keeping this kind of secret from him. He thought deep down that part of him did hate her, but it wasn't something he was enjoying. He didn't want to feel like that about her. She'd betrayed him, *hurt him* like nothing in his life had before, and although he knew it would be almost impossible to completely trust her again, damn it but he wanted to try.

The urge to yell and curse had passed, Gus had seen to that when they'd talked, but anger wasn't something that could just be forgotten. But it was starting to fade, more a dull ache now than a bone-deep fury. And part of him knew that he had to take some of the blame. He *had* always made his thoughts on parenthood blatantly obvious. He had left her behind and moved on with his life, even though he'd known there was more between them than just friendship. But then deep down he'd never really thought he was good enough for her. He'd grown up since then, realized what kind of man he was and what he wanted, but back then he hadn't.

His mind was a jumble of thoughts and he needed to get outside. *Outside with my horses, and away from Rebecca.*

Lexie appeared behind her mother and Ben forced the smile back on his face. He didn't want their daughter to see them arguing, not when it was the first time he'd actually spent time with the kid.

"You ready?" Ben asked.

Lexie looked down at her feet and shrugged. Ben stifled a laugh and bent down, putting the girl's hand on his shoulder to balance her, then removing each shoe and putting it on the correct foot, hands shaking. He laced them up, wishing just the simple act of helping her on with her shoes didn't put the fear of God in him.

He knew Rebecca was watching them, and as Lexie reached for his hand, he closed his eyes. His daughter had just felt comfortable enough to put her small hand in his, and her skin was warm and sticky, probably still covered in some of her breakfast. Soft and innocent in a way that an adult's skin just wasn't anymore—hell, his probably felt rough as anything to her. It took every inch of his willpower not to tug his hand out, because nothing about holding on to her felt any kind of natural.

Ben turned back to Rebecca. Tears welled in her eyes that he didn't want to acknowledge. He didn't want to dig the knife deeper, he *wanted* to let go, but a familiar pool of anger was beginning to form behind his eyes again, and he just couldn't help himself.

"I don't know why you kept this from me, Rebecca," he said, voice low, barely more than a whisper. "Honestly, I just don't understand." Lexie wouldn't know what they were talking about, he wasn't saying anything that would upset the girl, but he needed Rebecca to know. She'd hurt him badly, and it wasn't something he could just take on board and move on from that easily.

Rebecca was watching them, tears soundlessly streaming down her cheeks as she stared at Lexie holding his hand. "I'm sorry," she said. "I'm sorry a thousand times over."

Something changed in Ben then, something that he hadn't even known he was capable of. Because he knew. He knew then, without a doubt, from the emotion written all over her face and the pain in her eyes, that it wasn't because she'd wanted to hurt him that she'd done what she'd done. That when she'd told him she was trying to protect him, and do the best for their daughter, that without a shadow of doubt she'd meant it. But he'd had a right to know, to make his own decision about being involved in Lexie's life, and what he wanted was his daughter, to be her dad. Right now it was the only clear thing in his seriously screwed-up thoughts. But then maybe if he hadn't had the time away, hadn't had the chance to grow and follow his dreams, he wouldn't be feeling like this.

Lexie must have heard the catch in her mother's voice and turned, dropping Ben's hand when she realized her mom was crying.

"Mommy, what's wrong?"

Rebecca wiped at her eyes and braved a smile. Lexie stood in front of her, her eyebrows pulled together, worried about her mom. Rebecca gave her a quick hug before pressing their foreheads together, eyes on hers as she gave her a look that seemed to reassure her that everything was okay.

"I'm just excited about you going out to see the horses, that's all."

"Really?" Lexie asked, clearly not entirely convinced.

"Yes, really. You go for it, cowgirl."

As Lexie scooted toward the door she squared her shoulders and stood, taking a few steps toward Ben. The look on her face was different now; she wiped her tears away and took a visibly deep breath as he watched her.

"I did what I thought was right, Ben," she said, wrapping her arms around herself as she stared straight into his eyes. "I know now that it wasn't, and when I said last night that I'd do the same thing all over again? That I wouldn't change anything? I was lying. I'd tell you in a heartbeat, Ben." She forced her lip to stop quivering. "As soon as I saw you with her, I knew it was the wrong thing. That you needed to be the one to make that decision. But at the time all I could think about was protecting her and not holding you back."

"You're a great mom," he said, staring straight at her, wanting to wrap her into a big hug and tug her hard against him. “But you’re one hell of a lousy friend.”

Rebecca sighed. “Yeah. I was. And for the record, you would have been a great dad.”

He didn’t like the past tense. “I’ll make up for it,” he said, surprised by how deep and raspy his voice was. “She ain’t growing up without a dad, not anymore.” What he needed was to know when they were going to tell her, but he didn’t want to argue. They could take it one step at a time. *Starting now.* Which would give him the chance to figure out how to act naturally around her, how to just be himself and not be scared of her as if she was some fragile doll that he could break.

He was home, and now he had a daughter, and that meant he had to grow the hell up and accept his responsibilities. He wasn’t ever going to make the same mistakes his mother had; his child was going to come first, there was no other option acceptable to him.

Ben walked out the door and found Lexie

standing on the porch, her eyes trained on his, excitement just about bursting from her.

"Come on, Ben!"

He grinned and took her hand, letting her enthusiasm rub off on him. He'd always been terrified of being a dad, but suddenly being with Lexie, having her hand in his, was the most exhilarated he'd felt in ages. *Except for having Bec in his arms the other night.* He still had no idea what to do with her, how to act, but he was darn well going to try.

CHAPTER TWELVE

BEN PROPPED LEXIE up on the side of the corral and laughed at the serious look on her face. The kid was so excited she looked as if she could hardly breathe.

"You sit there, darlin'," he told her, putting one hand on either side of Lexie's legs and bending to look her in the eye. "I'm gonna bring Willy around so you can have a ride."

Lexie's eyes were open so wide they were about to pop. Ben gave her a wink and spun around to go get the horse.

"No running away, okay?" he called.

She was cute—shy but quietly determined. He liked that about her.

He caught Willy and gave the horse a scratch as they walked, watching Lexie as she kicked her legs against the timber she was sitting on.

"Lexie, I'd like you to meet Willy."

She looked nervous, her bottom lip grabbing under her top teeth. He hesitated then reached out for her when he saw her wobble, not sure how to touch her. She was so tiny and cute, he just didn't know what to do.

"Have you ever patted a horse before, Lexie?"

She shook her head and Ben tried not to freeze when she looped an arm around his neck so he could swing her down, just tried to behave as naturally as she was. She kept her legs firmly locked around his hips so he couldn't let her go, taking the initiative. It was reassuring to know he could just follow her lead.

"He's a real sweetheart, this one. And he loves to be stroked just here," Ben said, laughing when she gave him a superfast touch to the nose. "You know, your mom rode Willy just the other day."

Lexie turned to look at Ben, her brown eyes so innocently turned upward in question, as though she didn't believe that her mom had ever ridden a horse, let alone this one. Then she went back to tentatively touching Willy's nose, before letting her hand drift a little higher to touch the horse on the forehead.

"I thought you and I could go for a ride together on Willy. You can sit up front and we can go for a wander around the farm."

"Okay." Her voice was so quiet it was almost a whisper.

Ben popped her back up on the fence, tied Willy up a little bit farther away and hurriedly put on the horse's saddle and bridle. He'd worry about brushing him down later. He gave him a quick pat and untied his rope, turning back to Lexie.

"So I'm gonna lift you up nice and slow, then I'll hop up behind you."

He went to scoop Lexie up but received a quivering-lipped look that told him he was about to have a crash course in how to deal with tears if he didn't do something fast. He stared at her, trying to figure out what the heck he was supposed to do.

"Ah, how about I hop on first then lift you up?"

Lexie nodded and Ben quickly did exactly that, mounting, then reaching down for her. He hauled her up so her tiny body fitted snugly against his. She tucked back tightly against him, resting her head against his chest as he kept one hand pressed firmly to her, the other looped through the reins.

"You okay, sweetheart?"

She nodded, the movement gentle against his chest. "Uh-huh."

Ben bent his head to talk into his daughter's ear, tried to just do what felt natural to him. He so desperately wanted to whisper to her, to tell her he was her dad, that she had a father who loved her, but he didn't. *Couldn't.* No matter how angry he was with Rebecca, he wanted it to be right. *He wanted to get this right.* Finding out she had a dad was special, and it wasn't something he wanted to muck up. Although finding out he had a dad who wanted him would have been a bonus no matter how it had happened where he was concerned. He'd spent the latter half of his teens desperate to find his father, and when he had finally tracked down the guy who was biologically related to him, it had been the worst thing he'd ever done. His mom was lousy, but his father didn't even want to acknowledge he existed.

"Lexie, riding's all about relaxing," he told her. "Sit back against me, feel every step the horse takes. I want you to feel safe up here. There's nothing to fear."

He felt Lexie's body soften slightly. Her head knocked back again to rest on Ben's chest, which sent his heart thumping overtime. They rode like that for a few minutes, just circling around the large round pen.

"You feeling it?"

"Yup."

"You sure?" he asked, starting to relax himself, no longer so worried about having her body against his, being in charge of someone so tiny.

"Yeah, Ben," she said, wriggling against him. "I'm feelin' it."

He chuckled and pulled her closer to him, before steering Willy out of the yard so they could ride out over the farm. He was pretty sure he'd just fallen head over heels in love.

* * *

Rebecca was shaking, her entire body as nervous as a bunch of keys jangling. She'd decided there was nothing more terrifying than seeing her daughter sit on a horse, followed very closely by the terror of knowing her little girl was sitting with her father. Would Ben tell her? How would Lexie react? She knew her daughter would be thrilled to have a dad, but what did it mean for them? Would Ben ever trust her or want to be around her again? Would he go for joint custody? Her body shuddered as she took a deep, worried breath.

She'd started out watching them from a distance, standing on the porch, on the one hand nostalgic about what could have been, on the other so scared of what was going to happen next. She and Ben had been so close, almost as if they were on the cusp of reuniting, living in a fantasy world where she didn't have some massive lie she was keeping from him. And the night they'd had? She groaned just thinking about it.

When she thought of Ben, her mind was full of

memories, all of them good except for the way she'd hurt him the day before. Riding, yes, but so many other things, too. They'd had so many first times together: a stolen pack of cigarettes from Gus they'd smoked till they were blue in the face—to her knowledge neither of them had touched a cigarette since, but she remembered that day with a smile; they'd gotten drunk together for the first time; learned how to play polo, how to start a horse under saddle. The point was, they had been together every one of those times.

She and Ben went back so far. Sticky fingers from cola and hotdogs at the local fair, red faces from nasty sunburn, sitting out by the river talking, star-fished on the grass. There had been a time they'd shared everything, talked about everything, been everything to one another. *Been friends.*

And now she'd ruined it. But she had to think about it with no regrets. She was a mother now, her priority had been her daughter ever since she'd given birth to her. Losing out on a chance to be with Ben was a result of what she'd kept from him, and now Lexie had to be her number one. She might have thought Ben would never come home, not after all this time, but the past was the past. Lexie was her future, because she was fairly certain Ben would never forgive her enough for them to go back to where they'd been, to even be friends again, let alone the lovers they'd been only a week ago.

She heard the gentle clip-clop of hooves on the hard packed earth and raised her eyes again. Rebecca had become so engrossed in her thoughts she'd dropped her head and been gazing at her own toes. Willy was coming her way, and that meant she knew where Ben was heading. He was off toward the river, the place they'd always raced to on his crazy polo ponies.

Ben had his head dipped low, talking to Lexie, her little girl smiling with one of her hands on the reins, Ben's large ones covering hers. For a guy who hadn't known what the hell to do with the little girl a short time ago, he looked pretty at ease now.

She was on the bottom step of the porch now

and Lexie saw her. She took one hand off the pommel and waved fiercely to her, a grin from one ear right to the other.

"Hey, honey," she called.

Her heart was screaming out, she wanted nothing more than to pull her down and protect her, but she knew Lexie was in good hands. Ben was one of the best horsemen she knew, and if her girl was safe on any horse, it was on a horse with Ben. *Lexie's dad*, she thought. It just didn't sound right. Even though she'd known all this time, it had seemed more like a dream. A fantasy. But Daddy was most certainly back in their lives.

As she waved Lexie on, with her so gleefully smiling and waving back, Rebecca sucked down her pride and glanced at Ben. The look she received in return sent prickles spiking over her entire body. They rode by, but Ben's eyes never left hers—a piercing gaze that conveyed everything. *His hurt, his disappointment, his distrust*. But there was something else; the anger she'd seen in his gaze earlier seemed to have softened somehow, a look that made her hope…she sucked in a big lungful of air. She wasn't even going to think it, because she'd only end up heartbroken all over again.

All that mattered was that Lexie was smiling, and that from this day on, she'd have a dad who loved her. Lexie had always had a mom who'd do anything for her and grandparents who thought the world of her, but nothing would beat adding a dad to the mix. *Nothing.*

They still weren't back. It had been two hours since they'd left, and still they hadn't returned. Lexie would be starving hungry, grumpy as hell probably, and Ben should have known better than to take so long. Rebecca knew only too well that something could have happened…a snake bite, a fall, *anything*!

"That's not doing you any favors."

Gus's no-nonsense voice snapped her out of it. She looked up from her seat on the edge of the porch. Eyes that had been trained on the direction they'd left in finally taking a break.

"That worrying. It's no good," Gus said.

"They've just been a long—"

"They're fine." He gave her a sharp look and sat down beside her.

Rebecca started to cry and Gus didn't even attempt to comfort her. She sat there with tears dripping steadily down her cheeks and he didn't say a word until she'd sucked all her sadness back and cleared her throat.

"What you did was wrong, girl," he said, his voice even deeper than she'd remembered it all these years.

She nodded. She'd had a feeling Ben would have confided in him, but knowing she'd let Gus down hurt, too. Seeing him again now, she knew he deserved to be a grandfather. He had been so great to her, and Lexie would have enjoyed spending time with him. It was all such a mess, and the worst part was that it was all her doing. She'd tried so desperately to do the right thing, and all she'd done was make everything a hundred times worse than it had to be.

"You were young, Ben was leaving," he said, before making a deep grunting noise in his throat.

"Bad choices, but I can understand. They weren't choices you'd have made if he'd been home or you'd been able to go with him. Not to mention the two of you needed your heads banged together for not seeing that you were supposed to be more than friends."

Rebecca looked up, hardly able to believe what he was saying.

"You can?"

"Yes, Rebecca. I can." He turned to face her. "But I'm not the one you have to convince."

As if on cue, the trio appeared. Willy plodding along, Ben sitting straight, and her girl, *their girl*, slumped back. Fast asleep.

She looked over at Gus but he was gone, the light tap of the door falling shut signaling that he'd headed back inside again. Part of her wanted to flee before facing another discussion with Ben, but another part of her knew she had to face up to her decision and meet the consequences. Once the weekend was over, she was going to have to admit her lie to her family, and some of her friends, so things weren't exactly going to get any easier.

* * *

There was an awfully strained feeling between them, despite them both trying their best for Lexie's sake. Rebecca watched Lexie as her eyes drooped slightly, despite continuing to munch on her sandwich. The kid was starving, but once her blood sugar levels were restored, she'd be bouncing off the walls again.

"You want a nap?" Rebecca asked, as Lexie stuffed the last piece into her mouth.

"Uh-uh," she managed, her cheeks bulging like a little chipmunk settling in for winter. "Ben told me I could meet the foals."

She looked his way and Ben just shrugged. Rebecca knew better than to say no without softening her response, especially when Lexie was having so much fun, so she tried her best to talk around it.

"Maybe later sweetheart."

"Why?"

"Because the foals need a midafternoon nap, too. They're only babies, remember."

That seemed to satisfy her, and she managed to

get her upstairs and settled in for a sleep, tucking her up in bed with a blanket pulled up to her chin. She stroked her head and stared down at her, watching as she drifted off to sleep, before heading back to face Ben. He was thumbing through the paper, but she could tell he wasn't really interested. He was turning the pages too fast to actually be reading them.

"We'll be heading off later this afternoon."

Her words seemed to cut through the invisible barrier he'd erected between them.

"When?" he asked, looking up.

"Doesn't matter when, so long as we're home before dark. I have to work tomorrow."

Ben nodded and went back to flicking through the paper. It was so unlike him to be rude, to be so distant. She had no idea what to do. Rebecca felt more alone now somehow than ever before. Worse than being without a loving man by her side giving birth, worse than thinking Lexie would resent her for not giving her a two-parent family, just the pits. It was like watching from above, not actually being part of the scene unfolding before her.

Because in all the years she'd known Ben, all the times they'd been through, she'd never known him to be so resentful, so angry, so brooding.

"Lexie wanted to know when she could come here again. When she'd be able to stay for longer," Ben said, the fact that he was talking to her taking her by surprise.

"What did you say?" she asked.

"I said sometime soon." He met her gaze. "But what I should have said was all the time."

"You can't keep blaming me," she said, refusing to be the bad guy forever. "You know now, so the only thing left to do is figure out how we're going to make this work. I was wrong, I was stupid, but I can't take it back."

"The only reason I know, *Rebecca*, is because you were forced to tell me." Ben ground out his words.

He stood up and went to walk outside, his fists balled at his sides as he moved farther away from her.

"I loved you, Ben," she said to his back. "I loved you then and I love you now, and that's exactly why I didn't tell you. You want the truth? Well that's it. But the day you came back there was no doubt in my mind that I had to tell you, it was just a matter of when. *And how.*"

When he kept on walking, not stopping to look back, not acknowledging her words, not saying anything, she realized it was over. If he was going to forgive her, he would have done it by now.

Rebecca ran up the stairs to the bedroom. Lexie had her arms flung out, in deep sleep, but she couldn't wait for her to wake. Instead, she threw their things into the two bags she had, not stopping to fold, just getting everything of theirs packed and ready to go. It only took her one trip down to fill the car, then she was back upstairs, pulling Lexie into her arms.

She murmured, eyes half-open, and Rebecca smiled bravely down at her. It took her only a moment to put her in the car, fixed into her seat, and then she was behind the wheel. It was time for her to go home and give Ben some space.

CHAPTER THIRTEEN

REBECCA WATCHED LEXIE as she zoomed around with her cousins. Her brother, Ryan, and his wife, Lucy, had twin boys and they ran her girl ragged. They had a blast together all the time, and it wasn't as if she was planning on giving Lexie any siblings, so it was the perfect balance. She couldn't imagine letting anyone else close to them, let alone marrying a man and having more children. And now that she'd ruined everything with Ben… She shook her head, trying to push him from her mind. Being with him the other night had made her hope, *yearn*, for more, but she'd always known what the reality was going to be.

The atmosphere was relaxed and happy, as it always was when her family got together, and that's what she had to focus on. Now that her parents had retired and left her to the day-to-day running of the restaurant, they either enjoyed long days looking after their grandkids, putting on family lunches, or traveling around Australia. She wouldn't give up their Sundays together for anything—family meant everything to her, and if she hadn't had them she had no idea how she'd have pulled through the last few years.

And then she was back to Ben again. She took a deep breath, watching the kids as they ran around the backyard. Every second she had to herself, every moment of not doing something, was spent thinking about him. About the way she'd left, about the look on his face when he'd been teaching Lexie to ride—*everything*. He'd been so awkward with her at first, but it hadn't taken him long to look more at ease.

Her dad called out from the barbecue and she gathered herself up, cringing when she realized her bottom was wet from the grass.

"Meat's ready!" her father hollered, in case they hadn't heard him the first time.

Rebecca's mother appeared at the open door to

the house, carrying a big salad bowl. She smiled at her daughter as she passed and Bec felt nervous all over again. Today was the day she was going to tell them. The secret was out and it was time she told her family. The only reason she had hidden Lexie's paternity anyway was to shield Ben, but the lies were over now and she wanted to start fresh. They were her family and they'd be shocked, but they'd forgive her. *Unlike Ben.* Her mother would probably be more upset about the fact she'd kept it from him than from them.

The twins and Lexie came hurtling from their playhouse, and Rebecca scooped up a plate and took a sausage from the grill. Her father swatted at her but she managed to steal it anyway.

"You going to dish out for your two?" she asked her sister-in-law.

Lucy nodded and hauled up from her seat. Rebecca's brother cast her a watchful stare from his spot near the table, and Rebecca followed his gaze, seeing that it was his wife he was keeping a close eye on. Lucy was heavily pregnant and from the look of it he was in full alpha protective mode. It was a look she'd never had cast in her direction before, and she wished she had.

She pushed the thoughts away, ones she'd long since forgotten about that were somehow rising to the surface again, and took a slice of bread, squirting tomato sauce over it before wrapping it around the sausage. Lexie stood at her side, waiting like a drooling Labrador for her lunch.

"Why don't you take this back to the play-house?" she suggested.

Lexie nodded and reached for the plate, grinning up at her.

"What about Leo and Sammy?" Lexie asked.

Rebecca looked at her cousins and smiled. The boys were slightly older than Lexie, loved her to pieces and always included her in their games.

"Their mommy will get theirs," Rebecca said, licking some sauce from her finger that must have slipped from the bottle when she'd squeezed it "No running with food in your mouth!"

She skipped away anyway, Rebecca's words lost to the excitement of racing away from the adults.

Rebecca took her place at the table that covered the deck and fiddled with the edge of her napkin. This was going to be hard. Around her, the others were tucking in. Lucy was heaping her plate high with food, her mother was fussing over the salad and her dad was dishing steak on to everyone's plates, chargrilled just like always. Only her brother was actually looking at her. Ryan sat across the table, his eyes trained on her, eyebrows raised as he asked her a question without even saying anything.

"Did you have fun at the polo? Or was it all work and no play?" asked Lucy.

Bec smiled, digging her fingernails into her palm. It was now or never.

"It was busy, but good." She was conscious of all the faces now looking her way, everyone listening to her. "We served a lot of food and the crowd seemed to love it, and then I had a catch-up with, ah, Ben."

"Sorry we couldn't help out," Lucy continued, still serving herself food. "Next time you can count on me." She patted her stomach and made them all laugh. "Next year I'll be begging for a day at the polo! I'll just have to leave your brother behind with the kids."

"Must have been nice catching up with Ben again." Her mom made that clucking sound she did whenever Ben's name was mentioned, and Rebecca stifled a groan. They'd loved him like a son, which was why telling them was going to be even harder.

"Bec, are you okay? You seem kind of…" Ryan was staring at her, the question still on his lips. When she glanced at his plate and saw he hadn't touched his food, she knew he wasn't going to let it go. He knew something was up.

She took a deep breath and ran her tongue lightly over her lips. Her mouth was so dry it was like it was full of cotton candy. But here she was, surrounded by the people who loved her most, and she needed desperately to get this off her chest.

Rebecca looked over to make sure Lexie wasn't near, but she could hear their excited shrieks from the back fence. She turned back to see everyone waiting, watching her. It wasn't as if she was often the center of attention and she hated it.

"I, ah, well…" She hesitated.

Her mother placed her fork back on the table. Every sound, every look, was sending Rebecca's pulse rate higher. She closed her eyes for a moment and drew on all the courage she had.

"As you all know, I've been spending some time with Ben. He's back in Australia for good."

"Oh, that's wonderful news." Her mother beamed at her. "It'll be so nice for you two to reconnect some more."

At least Rebecca could count on her brother for picking up on her feelings—he was giving her a weird look again.

"Anyway, what I'm trying to say is that while I was there, I had to tell Ben something that I've kept from him and from all of you."

That stopped her mother from saying anything else. Rebecca blinked away tears, refusing to break down.

"Ben is Lexie's father." She said it so fast she wondered if they'd heard. But a glance around each face saw there was no mistaking it. They'd heard all right. Only no one was saying anything.

"*What?*" Ryan's face had turned a deep red and he thumped his fist down hard on the table, the first to react.

The clatter of cutlery made Rebecca jump. Her brother hadn't taken the news of her having a baby on her own well back then, so hearing that it was Ben's would have come as a shock. Probably a bigger shock to him than to her parents.

"Before you all jump to conclusions," she said, looking firmly at Ryan, "I want you to know that Ben didn't know. I only just told him, so there's no need to make him out to be the bad guy. If anyone is to blame, it's me."

Her mother looked as if she might cry, her father was back to fussing with the meat, and Ryan was still glaring at her.

"You're telling me that Ben McFarlane left you when you were pregnant?"

Rebecca looked sideways, not wanting to deal with her brother all hot under the collar. Lucy had her lips pursed, and she at least hoped her sister-in-law would be able to keep her brother calm.

"Ben had no idea I was pregnant when he left," she told him. "Had he known, he would have stayed. I can promise you that."

"So when are you getting married?" Ryan asked.

That made her laugh, although the noise died in her mouth when she saw the serious look on her brother's face.

"Ryan, I'm not marrying him!" she insisted. "We haven't even told Lexie yet. It's kind of difficult." She shook her head. "And that's why I didn't tell him in the first place, because he *would* have married me, out of a sense of duty, and the last thing I wanted was Ben giving up his dreams for me and resenting me for having to be tied to us." Not to mention the fact that she'd never really believed she deserved him, that she was worthy of him when she couldn't even face her own fears of getting back on a horse, of trying harder to make the team she'd dreamed about for years.

"I guess she does look like Ben, when you

think about it," her mother said, as if she was having a conversation with herself.

"I can't believe you lied to us all this time. All that garbage you spun about..."

Rebecca shook her head and stood up from the table, interrupting her brother.

"You know what? I shouldn't have lied, but I don't owe any of you an apology. The only person I need to say sorry to is Ben, and God only knows I've said that to him a hundred times over these past few days. But Lexie is my daughter, and who her father is, was my business. *Is* my business."

She stormed past the table and fled into the house, rushed into the bathroom and burst into tears. She had never spoken to her family like that, *never*, and she hated that she just had. The truth was, she *was* sorry. Sorry to everyone she'd hurt for not telling them the truth. But was she so bad to have wanted to protect her own daughter? To protect Ben and her own heart, too? Was she that terrible to want to let Ben go and live out his dreams? Because once upon a time they'd been her dreams, too.

A light knock on the door made her haul in a big sob and dab at her eyes.

"Honey, let me in. *Please.*" Her mother's soft voice made the urge to cry even greater.

She swung open the door and fell into her mother's arms, holding on tight and sobbing, her body shaking as she cried and cried. Rebecca felt like a child again, enveloped in her mother's comforting embrace.

"It's okay, honey. No one's angry with you. It's okay."

She knew Ryan wouldn't take long to forgive her, but her mother was wrong. There was someone angry with her, and the way her heart was slowly shattering, piece by piece, told her she'd blown it. Anything that might have been between her and Ben was well and truly over. She'd hurt him so badly and she just wanted to make it right. She wanted *him.* Not just as a friend, but as her something more, as the loving father of her child and as her lover.

Her mother held her tight in her arms, rocked her back and forward like Rebecca did to her own daughter to comfort her. It was not something she'd ever thought her mom would have to do to her again.

"It's going to be okay," her mother soothed.

"I love him," Rebecca choked. "I love him so bad."

"I know, sweetie," she said, and sighed. "I know. You loved him then, you always did."

"But I love him now, too. I never stopped."

Rebecca squeezed her eyes shut and willed Ben's face, his touch, his scent, to disappear from her memories. She'd never stopped loving him, and now, when she had almost had him back, she'd lost him forever. And it was all her fault.

The sun was beating down hard on Ben's bare arms, but he wasn't going to give up. He was sweltering from the heat, sweat pouring from his skin, and he was determined to keep going.

"Ben!"

He heard Gus call out to him, but he refused to

listen. He only needed a few more minutes, another half hour maybe, and he'd have cracked the filly. She was still dancing around him, snorting in that arrogant little way of hers, teasing him before skipping away. But if there was one thing he was, it was determined.

"Ben!"

The voice was closer this time. He still ignored it, until a firm hand fell on his shoulder.

"Enough."

The word took a moment to filter through his senses, but the continued pressure on his shoulder made him stop.

"I said, enough,' the slow, steady voice was unrelenting.

Ben turned slowly and looked at his grandfather.

"I want you to get out of here, and don't work with another horse until you've cleared your head."

He bit back a retort, and he was pleased he had. Gus didn't need to be on the sharp end of his tongue, just because he felt lousy. And besides, his grandfather was right. He should never have come out here expecting to work with the young filly in this frame of mind. He knew better, and Gus shouldn't have had to remind him.

Ben gave the filly a look he hoped conveyed his remorse, and exited through the wooden rails. Gus went the long way, walking through the gate. It wasn't that he'd been too hard on her, but he wasn't being patient enough, soft enough to a horse that needed gentle coaxing.

"What do you want, son?"

Ben closed his eyes for a second before turning to watch his grandfather. What he needed was a way to push all the thoughts running through his head away, to just inhale the fresh air out on the farm and give himself a break.

"I said, what do you want?" his grandfather repeated.

Clearly the old man wasn't in one of his chilled out moods. He was asking a question and he expected an answer.

"I don't know."

"Yes, you do," Gus replied. "You know exactly what you want, son. You just need to admit it."

He watched Ben, the two of them looking at one another for a long moment, before walking off with the assistance of his cane. Gus called over his shoulder.

"I'm going to get us a beer. Think about your answer."

Ben sat on the veranda and held the beer bottle against his forehead. The wet, cool feel was helping to reduce his body temperature, but it wasn't helping his thoughts any. He could sense his grandfather's eyes on him, and he knew he had to say something. If he couldn't tell Gus, who could he tell?

"I want Lexie to know I'm her father. I want my daughter." He sucked back a breath, then blew it out slowly. "I want to know how to act around her, just figure out how to be her dad."

Gus nodded. He took a slow swig of his beer, his eyes not leaving Ben's.

"What else do you want?"

Ben shrugged, but his aloofness wasn't fooling Gus. They sat in silence, the only noise the whinny of horses in the distance, and the odd chirp of a bird in the big trees surrounding the house.

"I want Rebecca, okay? I bloody darn well want Rebecca." Ben pushed up to his feet and stormed the length of the veranda, before rounding on his grandfather. "Is that what you wanted to hear?"

Gus just smiled at him.

"You're an idiot, you know that?" Ben glowered at Gus's words. "Get in that car and don't come back until you've told her."

Ben put his beer down and walked toward his granddad. He suddenly had this feeling that he wouldn't know what to do without Gus around, that he couldn't bear the thought of life without him. His age had caught up to him fast, and it scared the hell out of Ben.

"Come here you old pain in the neck."

Gus stood and they embraced. The kind of firm, strong hug that men shared when it really meant something. The kind of hug Ben had always been able to count on, when he was a little boy to right now as a fully grown man. The type of support every human being needed in life.

"Call *me* a pain in the neck?" Gus chuckled. "You've been like a bear with a thorn, boy."

Ben grinned.

"You know that little pony we talked about?"

"I'm on it," said Gus.

"Great. I'm gonna head into town and see if I can't get them both back here."

CHAPTER FOURTEEN

THE RESTAURANT WAS BUZZING, which made it easier for Ben to slip in unnoticed. He'd gone straight to Rebecca's house, but then figured she'd be working.

It had always been busy, but it felt different now. He wondered if it was Rebecca's touch, making it that much more special, more intimate, than it had been previously. It had always been one of inner-city Melbourne's busiest Italian restaurants, but the subtle changes made it even more appealing.

Ben kept his head down and sat at a vacant table. He was a bundle of nerves and he hated it. He toyed with the menu but his eyes just skimmed over the words. He didn't care what he ate. For the first time in as long as he could remember he wasn't even interested in food. All he cared about was the woman he'd come here to see.

"Would you like to hear the specials?"

He looked up into pretty blue eyes. *Not Rebecca.* He didn't want to offend the young woman, so he politely said no and just ordered the spaghetti Bolognese. If Rebecca wasn't the one to bring his lunch over, he'd just eat and drink coffee until the rush had died down.

Ben watched the hum of people, coming and going, listening to laughter and conversation, but all he wanted was to see Rebecca. His eyes danced over each table, then out to the kitchen, scanning for her. *And then he saw her.*

Rebecca emerged, holding two steaming plates of food, held high out to each side. Her golden blond hair was pulled back into a loose ponytail, and it swished behind her as she moved. Her mouth was tipped up at each corner into a smile, and she looked happy. He hoped she'd still have that sweet look on her face when she saw him.

He let his eyes follow her as she hurried to a table and placed the two plates down, before saying a few words and heading back to the kitchen. Ben exercised all his willpower to stay seated, when all he wanted to do was take off after her.

His gaze stayed trained on the kitchen, and this time he was rewarded more quickly when she appeared again almost straight away, this time holding only one plate. Ben sat back, trying to look relaxed. She was heading his way. Ten steps, eight, six… She saw him.

Rebecca locked eyes with him, her mouth turning heart shaped with surprise. She looked over one shoulder, and then at the plate, as if wanting it to be a mistake. She hesitated. Ben rose to his feet.

"I think that's my spaghetti."

She still looked stunned, so he walked the few steps to meet her and took the plate for himself.

"Can you sit a minute?" he asked.

She shook her head, looking as though she was about to take off in the other direction.

"Please."

"I can't," she stammered. "We're so busy and I need to get more orders to tables."

He watched her, eyes bonded on hers, and then nodded.

"Okay. I'll wait."

Rebecca took a few steps backward before rushing off in the direction of the kitchen. Ben sat down and tried to approach his meal with interest, but his stomach was growling with a different type of hunger. Now that he'd seen her again, he wanted her. Badly. And this time he wasn't going to let anything get in their way. She'd apologized to him enough and it was time to put the past in the past and claim his family. He'd wasted enough time without wasting even more behaving like an idiot.

He'd left her once, walked away when he knew in his heart that he shouldn't have gone without telling her how he truly felt, but now he was back. For good. And there was nothing, *nothing*, going to stand in his way.

There were only a handful of patrons left. Ben pushed his coffee cup away. It was his third and he had enough caffeine in his system to keep him alert for days.

He'd watched Rebecca walk back and forth from the kitchen, smiling her way around each table, and now he was waiting for her to reappear. She'd disappeared out back a few minutes ago and not reemerged. Part of him was worried that she'd done a runner out the fire exit, but he believed in her more than that. Hoped he could trust that she wouldn't just leave him.

But even if she did bolt, he'd track her down and make her hear him out. If she was worried about listening to him fume at her again, she was wrong—he was a big enough man to admit he hadn't dealt with finding out well, but he was going to make up for it now. He was going to be a great dad even if it terrified him; and if she let him, he was going to make up for lost time with her, too.

He smiled as Rebecca finally reappeared and walked toward him—she hadn't bailed after all. She was fiddling with her apron, playing with the edge, and when she got closer she held her hands behind her back and untied it. She was wearing dark denim jeans, ballet flats and a plain black T-shirt, and she looked great.

"Hey," she said.

Ben hadn't seen Bec blush in a long time, but her cheeks were as pink and flushed as he'd ever seen them.

"Hey," he said back.

He stood and pulled out a chair. She sat down, her hands still busy on the cotton of her apron, obviously trying to distract herself from the fact that he was there.

"I had to see you, Bec," he started, pleased when she finally looked up. "When you left like that the other day, I didn't know what to think."

She at least gave him a reaction then.

"What did you expect, Ben?" She kept her voice low but she was clearly angry. "You made it pretty clear you didn't want me around."

"Bec…"

This wasn't going well. He'd come in here knowing exactly what he wanted to say, had practiced the entire conversation while he was waiting for her, and now he could hardly get his words out.

"No, Ben, let me," she said. "I'm not going to say sorry again because you've made it pretty clear there's no chance of me being forgiven. So why are you here?"

He stayed quiet. She was wrong, but he could tell now wasn't the time to tell her otherwise. She had something to say and he was going to sit tight and let her say it.

"Lexie's your daughter, and you have every right to be part of her life. We can work out some sort of an arrangement, something that works for both of us. My family knows now, so it's all out in the open."

Ben nodded. "Where is she now?"

"At my parent's place. She had a little cold, so I let her hang out there all day instead of going to preschool."

"She's okay, though?"

Rebecca nodded and stood up. "Sorry if you came all the way in just to see her, but I've really got to help tidy up. I'm off tonight and I want everything ready for dinner service before I leave."

Ben stood, too. There was so much he wanted to say but clearly now was the wrong time. Wrong place. At least he'd been able to observe these past few hours. If he'd been unsure to start with, he was positive now.

He just needed to figure out how to show her how he felt, so she believed him when he told her that he loved her. It wasn't just because they had a daughter together, or because he wanted to be part of Lexie's life. He wanted Rebecca, whether they had a child or not. And by the end of the day there was no way she wouldn't know exactly what he wanted. *Her.*

Ben pulled his car up outside the Stewarts' place. He hadn't come here that much as a kid, he and Rebecca tended to spend all their time at the stables when they hung out, but he still knew it well.

There was a car he didn't recognize out front, but he could hardly wait until the guest had gone. He didn't have long before Rebecca arrived back, and he needed to talk to her parents before she came home. And he wanted to spend some time with his girl.

He crossed the road and took a deep breath. It was odd knowing that Lexie had no idea he was her father, but he was still desperate to see her. His mind had done nothing other than flick between Rebecca and Lexie for the past few days, and even thought it sounded stupid even in his own head, he'd missed her.

Ben pushed the doorbell and waited. It was only a few minutes before a heavily pregnant woman flung open the door.

"Hi," she said.

"Ah, hi," he said back. "This still the Stewarts' place?"

A scream and a thunder of feet took him by surprise. The woman laughed as three kids, all in various states of undress, ran down the hall toward them.

"Sorry," she said.

"Ben!"

He recognized Lexie straightaway when she

slid on the timber floorboards and screeched to a halt. At least he knew he had the right place.

"Hey, Lexie."

Lexie shot straight forward and grabbed his leg, her wet hair colliding with his chest when he bent down.

"What have you been doing?"

"Water fights," she said, shrugging. "I'm supposed to be sick, but I'm fine."

"You're Ben?"

The woman who'd answered the door had a warm expression on her face, smiling as she stared down at him.

"Sorry, Ben McFarlane," he said, standing and holding out his free hand. "And you are?"

"Lucy," she said, letting go and resting her hand on top of her belly. "Ryan's wife."

Ben nodded. "Can I come in?"

Rebecca turned the radio up loud and sung along. Badly. Seeing Ben today had been worse than when he'd first come back. She still felt such a fool for telling him she loved him, couldn't stop playing that day over and over in her mind. She'd managed to keep her feelings for him hidden for years, but now she seemed incapable of not making a mess of everything.

She pulled up outside her parents' place and noticed the black Holden next to the curb. The car looked a little too familiar. It only took a second before her heart hit the footpath. What was he doing here? Had he come for Lexie?

Rebecca rushed up the drive and pushed open the front door. He might only want their daughter, not her, but he couldn't just barge in like this and expect to take her!

"Mom!" she called. "Lexie!"

There was no one in the house. She rushed through the lounge and into the kitchen, worried something had happened. Where were they?

And then she saw the open doors leading out to the backyard and she was greeted with her worst nightmare. Ben was sitting beside her mother, both with chairs they had pulled out onto the grass. Lucy was fanning herself beneath a big tree, and her father was standing beside the water tap. Lexie was squealing with delight as she ran and then slid down some slippery, green, plastic water thing, and the twins were running back and forward with her. One would run and belly flop onto the plastic, then slide to the end, before the next child would start.

Rebecca looked at Ben. He'd obviously just said something funny, because he had her mother with her head thrown back in laughter. She felt physically sick. It was like some sort of weird setup.

"Mommy!"

Lexie was the first to notice her standing there. She gave her a wave and then shooed her away as she shook out water from her hair.

Ben jumped up and headed her way. Rebecca felt the urge to run, but forced her feet to stay rooted to the spot. He obviously hadn't come here to steal Lexie away, so what on earth was he doing?

"What are you doing here?" she asked, not wasting any time.

He gave her a big smile and shrugged.

"Not quite the welcome I was hoping for." He

reached for her arm but she angled herself so he didn't quite connect.

"Look, I get that you want to make up for lost time, but this is kind of hard for me," she told him.

"Rebecca..."

"No, Ben, don't bother. I shouldn't have lied. I know it's Lexie you want, not me, and I should have just kept my mouth shut."

"Rebecca."

She looked up and into his chocolate-colored eyes; eyes she'd dreamed about for months after he'd left, before she was able to just gaze into her daughter's.

"I need you to come with me. I've organized for your dad to run the restaurant tomorrow. I need you and Lexie to join me."

That knocked the wind out of her as if she'd been sucker punched.

"You have no right to come here and change my life around," she whispered, conscious that all eyes were on them. "I can't believe you think you can just rearrange me and tell me what to do."

"You know what, Bec?"

"What?" she fired back.

"Just shut up and do what I say for once. Okay?" He laughed. "And has anyone ever told you that you look damn gorgeous when you're all mad?"

She looked past him to see her mother grinning. She'd probably never heard anyone boss her daughter around like that before. Rebecca glared at her and turned her back. Just when she needed someone on her team her own family was swapping sides. She gave Ben what she hoped was an unimpressed stare, hands on her hips, but she had to admit it was nice seeing him joke around, laugh like that. It reminded her of the Ben of old.

"Fine," she snapped, although her anger was quickly dissipating.

Ben grinned and turned back to the kids.

"Lexie, last round, sweetheart. I've got a surprise for you," Ben called out, as if he was suddenly at ease with spending time with her, hanging out with the child he'd looked as good as terrified of when she'd first told him.

Rebecca shook her head and received only a

shrug of the shoulders from her mother. Conveniently her dad was still busying himself with the children's game. Lucy just gave her a thumbs-up and Bec glowered back at her. It was as if everybody but her knew what was going on and she didn't like it at all. She was always the one in control, planning to the last detail, organizing everybody else. Ben had no right to barge in here, into her family's home, and tell her what to do!

She looked back at her mother and her sister-in-law, then to Ben. They were all grinning like dummies.

This was definitely an ambush. She knew when she'd been outnumbered, and right now she was guessing those numbers were at least one hundred to one.

CHAPTER FIFTEEN

REBECCA DIDN'T LIKE SURPRISES, and she wasn't particularly pleased that Ben had spent time with her parents without discussing it with her first.

The car slowed and Rebecca refocused. She could hardly believe they were at McFarlane's all ready.

"Are we here?"

Lexie's sleepy voice broke the silence.

"Yup, we're here," Ben told her.

Was she the only one not happy? Ben had grinned the entire trip here, Lexie had chirped excitedly before falling asleep and was clearly back to her perky self again already, and she felt nothing but miserable. A wave of dread kept looping through her stomach, telling her something was wrong, but there was little she could do. Ben had made it clear he expected her to comply, and she was sick of arguing with him. Of feeling like everything was her fault. She simply couldn't be bothered fighting, saying no, especially with Lexie around. And the way she felt around him even though she knew nothing could happen? *Ugh*. Being in such close proximity to him wasn't doing her any favors.

When the car stopped she got out and helped Lexie, but her daughter made a beeline straight for Ben, trotting along beside him like a loyal puppy dog. So much for her clingy girl, she thought. Someone better came along and she was gone in a flash.

Rebecca wanted to feel happy that Lexie was going to have a dad in her life, she knew it was petty to think otherwise, but she couldn't help it. Ben was so clearly besotted with his child, and so appalled by her, she felt torn. It had been wrong not to tell him, she could see that now, but what more could she do than say sorry? If there was anything that could make things right between them, she'd do it.

"You coming, Bec?"

Ben calling out spurred her into action and she hurried after them.

"Come on, Mommy!" Lexie called.

She had soon caught up with them, catching a glimpse of Gus waving out, then disappearing into the stable. Something was definitely up. She had that feeling like everything was just too quiet, like some sort of set up.

"Are you ready for a surprise?"

Lexie nodded fiercely. If she'd nodded any harder her head would have fallen off.

Ben looked around to Rebecca. He gave her a look and pointed at Lexie. They stared at one another a long while, before she nodded. There was nothing else she could do, the message was conveyed so clearly in his eyes, his desperation clear for anyone to see.

She got it. He was going to tell Lexie that he was her dad. It upset her that they hadn't talked about it first, but she was Ben's daughter, and she guessed it was up to him to decide how and when he wanted her to find out. Ben walked toward her and she felt guilty for wanting to keep it from their little girl.

"You okay with me telling her?" Ben asked in a low tone, his mouth achingly close to her ear when he moved over, his hand closing over her forearm.

"Yes." What else could she say?

Ben beamed at her and whipped Lexie off her feet and up into his arms, as if he'd done it a million times before. He'd obviously decided he wanted to make a huge effort with her, and it showed.

"Lexie, today's a very special day. Do you know why?"

"'Coz I didn't have to go to preschool?"

Lexie squinted up at Ben, the sun in her eyes. Ben laughed and swung her, before hoisting her up onto his shoulders. Rebecca kept her distance. Her entire body was numb, her eyes wet, hands clammy. All she could do was watch, and feel her heart crumble into piece after piece. To an outsider, this would have looked happy, idyllic even. But the reality was Lexie had gained a father and she'd lost a friend. There was no chance for her and Ben to be anything other than civil parents, with no chance of a reconciliation. His feelings toward her had made that clear.

"Today's a special day because today you get to meet your dad." Rebecca listened to Ben's gruff, deep words as Lexie screwed her face up.

"Where is he?" Lexie asked.

Ben smiled. Rebecca didn't think she'd ever seen him look so happy. Not when they used to gallop down the beach, racing side by side on horseback; not when they used to sneak out and sit on the roof, talking for hours well into the night; *not ever.* She had never since she'd known him ever seen him look like that.

"I'm your dad, Lexie," Ben said simply. "It's me."

Lexie looked confused and Rebecca worried she didn't understand.

"How can you be my dad? You're Ben," Lexie asked.

"I know it's hard to understand, kiddo, but I

promise you that I'm your dad, and I'm always going to be. I'm your father, sweetheart."

Lexie wriggled and he pulled her down from where she was perched on his shoulders, putting her on his hip so she could look at both of them. Rebecca had tears in her eyes but she tried so hard to stop them from falling.

"Mommy, do you know that Ben is my dad?"

That made them both laugh. Rebecca just smiled, trying to look happy, watching as little Lexie sat back in Ben's arms to look up at him some more. Children were so innocent, she thought. Her darling wee girl was so kind, so sweet and loving, and looking at her in her father's arms did make her happy. She only wished that same man wanted them both in his arms, not just his daughter. That they could be the family she had secretly dreamed of all these years. It broke her heart to think that Ben would meet someone, someday, and that Lexie would be with her daddy and another woman.

"There's one more surprise."

Rebecca looked up. What else was going on?

Lexie was wriggling so much that Ben had to put her down. Just as he did so, Gus came slowly around the corner, leading the cutest, tubbiest little pony Rebecca had ever seen.

Lexie was dead still now. She was holding on to Ben but she wasn't moving.

"This, Lexie, is a present from your dad."

Rebecca watched as Lexie looked from the pony to Ben.

"Since you love horses so much, I thought you deserved your own pony. Especially if you're going to be spending time here."

Lexie zoomed forward. Thankfully the pint-size pony wasn't worried, and just stood as Lexie inspected every inch of him, touching, patting, talking to him all the while.

Ben left her to it, under Gus's watchful eye, and turned to Rebecca. His grandfather was grinning ear to ear.

"We need to talk," Ben said in a low voice. "Keen for a ride?"

Rebecca nodded, still numb.

"Come on, then."

She followed after him, hardly able to process what was going on. She had no idea what to expect, only for the first time all afternoon, she was starting to believe it might be something good. Something so good she didn't even want to admit it.

They rode in silence for a while. Rebecca had no idea where they were going, why she was here, or what Ben wanted to talk about. If he just wanted to talk custody arrangements? She swallowed hard. Surely he wouldn't be making such an effort if it wasn't something more…Rebecca shook her head, as if it would somehow make the thoughts disappear. What she needed to do was just stop thinking.

Ben stopped then. She halted behind him and waited for his lead.

"Let's get off here," he said before dismounting.

She was pleased at least that she had her old riding mojo back. Her brain might have been working overtime, but her body had been loving the easy motion of the horse's walk.

Rebecca followed his lead, wishing Ben had been guiding her down, like he'd helped her mount that first time she'd ridden with him again after he'd arrived home. She craved his hands on her body, palms firm at her hips, the steadiness of his hold on her. They were dangerous wishes, she knew that, but she couldn't help it and it was worse knowing it was never going to happen again. Besides, she didn't need his assistance now. She wasn't the same timid rider she'd been that first day back on the farm.

Ben took the reins from her and tied the horses to a low fallen tree trunk in the shade. The day was hot, but the sun was sitting lower now, a late afternoon breeze keeping the temperature bearable.

He sat down on the same big trunk and beckoned her over. Rebecca complied, keeping her distance from him. She still didn't know why they were here, what they were doing, and the last thing she needed was to be within touching distance to him.

"I hope you didn't mind me telling her back there?"

She shook her head. "She'll have a lot of questions later, once she's had time to process, but that's okay."

"So you're all right with it?"

"She's your daughter, Ben. You had every right to tell her."

"Not too extravagant with the pony?"

Ben was smiling and she smiled back. He was obviously very proud of the cute pony he'd bought, and he deserved to enjoy the moment.

"It was the best present a kid could wish for. It was very kind of you."

They sat a few more minutes. Rebecca was feeling incredibly uncomfortable. This might not be hard for him, but she'd thought about him every day since he'd left. Thought about him double as much since she'd stormed out the other day. Wishing things were different; wishing she'd just told him before ending up confessing the way she had. She just wished she could go back in time and change everything, but she couldn't and she just had to suck it up and get on with her life.

"You don't want to go for full custody or anything, do you?" The thought made her feel worse than sick. "I love her so much, Ben, and I just couldn't deal with…" She bit down hard on her lip, shaking her head. "I just want to protect her."

Ben didn't answer, but he did shuffle closer to her along the rough wood of the tree trunk.

"I didn't bring you out here to talk about Lexie. And I sure as hell don't want to take her away from you."

She looked up. "You didn't? *Wait, you don't*?"

Ben shook his head, his eyes looking straight ahead toward endless parched yellow grass.

"I wanted to tell you that I understand. I know why you did what you did, and I need you to know that I forgive you."

She went to answer but snapped her mouth back closed. *He forgave her?*

"I've had time to think these past few days, and it made me realize that I was a jerk. I was hurt, but I still should have listened to you, heard you out." He shrugged. "We were best friends, Bec. You were the one person in the world who always knew me as well as I knew myself, and I guess it was hard hearing what you had to say the other day, the fact that you knew how scared I was of ever being a parent, of what I'd been through. You were right, I just didn't want to admit to it."

"You had every right to treat me like that, Ben," she answered. "I never should have kept it from you. It was wrong, I know that."

Ben took her hand, and she fought not to pull it away. She didn't want his touch, his pity. Didn't want him to feel sorry for her. She just wanted to figure out how they were going to make this parenting thing work then get on with it. Hoping for something more was stupid, dangerous.

Ben held her hand tighter so she couldn't pull it away. "Did you mean it when you said you still loved me?"

Rebecca's heart collapsed, then kick-started again. She didn't trust her voice, didn't know if she could even force a word out.

"Did you?" Ben asked again.

"Yes," she stammered. There was no point in lying—she'd told him how she felt the other day and it wasn't as if anything had changed.

"Bec," he said, standing and pacing a few steps before coming back to stand in front of her, casting a shadow over her as he blocked out the dappled sun coming through the leaves.

"I'm sorry, Ben," she said, wanting nothing more than to fall to the ground and cry, to shatter into pieces and not have to re-form until he'd gone. "I wish I didn't but I do. I wish I could just want to be friends with you, but it'd be a lie."

"You've said sorry enough," he whispered, dropping to his knees. "I forgive you, Rebecca. *I forgive you.*"

She looked up, warmth slowly trickling back into her veins as she met his gaze.

Ben dropped to his knees and grasped her hands between his. She didn't know where to look. *What was he doing?*

"Bec, will you marry me?"

CHAPTER SIXTEEN

REBECCA SUCKED IN a sharp lungful of air. Marry him? *Was he kidding?*

"Ben, you can't be serious!"

His eyes didn't leave hers, his hands steady as he clasped hers, fingers linked together.

"I'm serious, Bec." He smiled, then repeated his question. "Will you marry me?"

She snatched her hands away from him, hating how desperately she wanted him, how badly she just wanted to throw herself into his arms.

"No," she whispered.

Ben stared at her, long and hard.

"What do you mean, *no*?"

She blinked back a gasp of unshed tears and jumped up, made her way to her horse. Willy stood patiently, but when she made a grab for his reins a heavy, firm grip stopped her. Ben's fingers dug into her arm, not letting her move another inch.

"Let me go." She tried to sound forceful but it came out as little more than a whisper.

"*No.*" Ben kept hold, his grip firm on her arm as he reached for her other wrist. His gaze made his intentions clear: there was no chance of him letting her go.

"You're not going anywhere."

"Let go of me, Ben." She fought hard, struggling to release herself. "Ben, you're hurting me!"

He let go of her wrist, his other hand softening over her arm.

"Why?" he asked.

Rebecca slumped against the horse, her resolve long gone. She turned sad eyes in Ben's direction.

"Same reason I didn't tell you about Lexie in the first place," she said sadly.

Ben looked confused, folding his arms across his chest as he stared at her.

"I didn't want you to propose back then just because you thought it was the right thing to do, and I don't want you to have to do it now. You don't owe me anything, Ben. You don't need to marry me out of some sense of, I don't know, duty."

"*Duty*? Is that honestly what you think?"

"Oh, I don't know," she said, trying hard not to cry. "Pity, then, whatever you want to call it. But you don't need to propose to me because you feel you have to."

Ben stepped toward her and placed a hand softly on each arm. She closed her eyes and tried to ignore the fact that he was touching her, of how good it felt to have his skin over hers. The man of her dreams had just asked her to marry him, was touching her, holding her, but it wasn't real, she knew that. She'd always known that he would step up if he knew, and here he was trying to make an honest woman of her.

"Rebecca, look at me."

When she didn't reply, he hooked one finger under her chin, forcing her to look at him. She swallowed, finally returning his gaze.

Ben didn't give her any warning. He crushed his lips hard against hers, taking her mouth with force. Rebecca tried to pull away, halfheartedly, before giving in and kissing him back. His hands were all over her, up and down her back, touching her hair, cupping her face. They stayed like that for what felt like hours, lost to one another's touch, lips locked, hands exploring, skin alight.

It was Ben who pulled back. He still had his hands around her waist, encircling her, keeping her locked in his cocoon.

"Did that feel like a man who pities you?" he asked. "Who thinks he has to marry you just because it's the right thing to do?"

She caught her lower lip beneath her teeth, still not wanting to hope that maybe she'd been wrong all this time.

"No," she managed to whisper in reply.

"I love you, Rebecca. I always have." He leaned in and pressed a soft, barely there kiss to her lips, his mouth hovering over hers. "And I always will. I should have told you years ago."

She let her eyes flutter shut for a moment, fighting the feeling that it was a dream. When she opened them again he was still there, his warm brown gaze locked on hers.

"I have always loved you, Rebecca. You have to believe me when I say I want you to marry me because I *still* love you, not because it's the right thing to do."

She nodded. It was all she could do. Her own voice had been taken captive in her throat.

"I want you to be my wife. I want to be Lexie's dad. And I want us all to be together." He sighed. "No pity. No sense of duty. Just because I damn well love you, Bec."

She looked up at him. His gaze was unwavering, hands strong on her hips as he held her gently in place.

"So, will you have me?" he asked.

"Yes," she murmured, the word drawing them closer together, her arms looping around his neck, letting herself believe that he actually did want her just for her. "Yes, Ben. Yes a million times over."

Ben pulled her in tight against him then, his lips falling to hers once more. She sighed into his mouth as he kissed her, before he trailed butterfly-soft kisses down her throat.

Rebecca moaned, her legs close to buckling beneath her. Ben didn't stop. He scooped her into his arms, his mouth back on hers. She shuddered as his tongue teased her lips, groaned as he dropped slowly to the ground and put her carefully on the grass.

He tugged his T-shirt off in between long, languid kisses, and Rebecca ran her hands over his strong back, felt his hard muscles coil and tense beneath her touch.

"I've been waiting to do this again for so long," he muttered against her lips.

Rebecca moaned beneath his touch. *So had she.*

"You are so beautiful," said Ben, holding her close.

She looked away, shy at being the object of his words but not wanting him to stop touching her, kissing her.

Rebecca closed her eyes and let Ben caress her. She had dreamed of this for so long, never thinking that one day she would be back in his arms. Back with the man she loved. She had gone all this time alone, with no other human being to keep her warm at night, to be her mate in life, to love, and now she had Ben, and she was never, ever going to let him go. Not if she could help it.

Ben traced a fingertip over Rebecca's skin, starting at her wrist then all the way up to her neck, and to her lips. Rebecca giggled and he dropped another kiss to her mouth.

"You are going to marry me, aren't you?"

She smiled at him, her mouth stretched wide, her face mirroring how he felt.

"Yes, I'm going to marry you, Ben McFarlane. A hundred times *yes*."

"Good."

"Good?" she repeated. "Is that all you think of me? *Good*."

He pinned her back on the grass, his mouth inches from her face, trying to be serious when all he wanted to do was laugh.

"Do you need me to show you again what I really think of you?" he growled.

Rebecca burst out laughing as he held her down.

"Okay, okay," she said, giggling.

Ben let her go and lay back down beside her, their bodies side by side. He kept hold of her hand, fingers interlinked.

"What do you think Lexie will make of us being together? Of me marrying her mom?"

"She already loves you, Ben," she said, squeezing his fingers. "I think she fell in love with you from the moment she met you, like she knew there was some sort of connection there."

Ben propped up on one elbow again, looking down at her. Her golden hair was fanned out around her over the grass and he stared down into eyes that had haunted him for years.

"You know what?" she asked.

"What?" He smiled as she stroked his arm, her touch featherlight.

"I think Lexie would have been happy with you in our lives even if you weren't her biological dad."

Ben opened his eyes. For all his worrying about being a father, of not wanting to screw up like his own mom had, he suddenly wasn't scared of being in Lexie's life. Maybe Bec had been right in letting him go at the time, even though it hurt like hell to admit it. He wanted to be Lexie's father—it was a belly-deep feeling that would be impossible to fight, but if he'd been faced with this before he'd been away, maybe it would have been harder to accept, to man up to. Maybe he wouldn't have realized how badly he wanted Bec as his partner instead of his friend, to be back on home soil, to make a life for himself on the land he'd grown up on.

"She's a great kid, you know?" His voice was hoarse with emotion.

Rebecca nodded her agreement. "Yeah, and you're going to be just as good a dad."

He hoped so. Man, did he hope so. "If I can be half as good a dad as Gus has been a grand-dad to me, then I guess I'll be fine." He blew out a breath. "I was so scared of her that first day, I didn't know what to do or how to even talk around her, but once I thought about how Gus was with me, it started to come more naturally."

She leaned up and kissed his jaw. Rebecca

crawled up into his arms and he tugged her tight, holding her close.

"I was so scared of being close to anyone, and in the process I somehow forgot that I was already close to you. I pushed you away when I should have kept you at my side. Made you a part of my life."

She sighed, head to his chest. "Does any of that matter now?"

"No," he whispered, kissing the top of her head. "Because I'm going to spend every day from this day forward making it up to you."

CHAPTER SEVENTEEN

REBECCA EYED THE beautiful black filly and bit down a lump of fear threatening to constrict her throat. She had been psyching herself up for this moment for days, but it didn't make it any easier.

She knew Ben was watching her but she didn't turn. He had offered countless times to help her, but this was something she had to do alone. There was no point becoming the first Mrs. McFarlane to take residence here since Ben's grandmother, without proving she could conquer her fear. Ben had been man enough to forgive her, to make her realize that she deserved his love, and that he was acting from his own feelings and not from duty. And now she owed it to herself to step up, take ownership of her past and believe in her own abilities. As a rider, as a woman and as an equal to him on the farm.

“Hey, Missy,” she soothed, leaving her fear on the other side of the corral. “How’s my girl today, huh?”

As if understanding her, the horse nickered and reached out her nose to run it over Rebecca’s forearm, tickling her bare skin.

Rebecca brushed Missy’s back, her hands moving along the indent of her shoulder, then down around her belly. Next she softly rubbed her face, before moving to place the saddle on her back. The horse didn’t move, and Rebecca gradually tightened the girth. When she moved to tease the bit into her mouth there was no hesitation, and she slipped the bridle over her head.

She glanced over her shoulder at her support crew and smiled. It was nice to see Gus and Ben standing there, but some of the polo guys who’d arrived were a little intimidating.

Rebecca talked in her low singsong voice to Missy and led her out to the center of the corral. A few strokes of the neck and tug of each stirrup later, and she was settling into the saddle.

Missy jumped and quivered, but Rebecca

stayed calmed. She kept talking, a running commentary of nonsense that made the horse relax and listen, ears flicking back and forth. Rebecca squeezed her legs and they moved forward at a slow walk. That was all she wanted from today, didn't want to push things too far.

It wasn't the most relaxing of rides, but Rebecca was proud of herself. A few weeks ago, she'd been scared of going near a horse again. Now? She couldn't deny having a belly full of nerves, but she was finding her way back to her past in the best possible way. She was a mom, she ran a restaurant, and now she was going to be Ben's wife, a wife who'd be confident back in the saddle with him, training for polo matches and having fun. She finally felt like *her* again.

Missy jumped beneath her but she just kept on talking, keeping a firm contact with the reins. Rebecca circled her and then pulled to a halt, before swinging her feet out from the stirrups. She praised the horse.

Nothing had turned out the way she'd expected, but she couldn't be happier. She looked across and met Ben's strong, unwavering gaze. When he grinned she blew him a kiss. She was finally with the man she loved, and nothing, *nothing*, could take that away from her.

Ben gave his grandfather a nudge, not even trying to wipe the beamer of a smile from his face. He'd always known she had it in her. There was something exciting about seeing his girl, his wife-to-be, sitting proud on a horse. Gus had known she could do it, he'd hoped she could do it, and eventually Rebecca had believed enough in herself to trust her instincts and give it a go again.

Nobody could have blamed her for being scared, for not wanting to try again, but she had, and he was pleased. He loved Bec, he loved his daughter, and he loved horses. Just thinking about training with her again, playing polo side by side with her, made him grin.

Ben jumped to his feet and moved toward his fiancée. It gave him a buzz just thinking about marrying her.

"Son?"

He turned and looked at his grandfather. Gus looked as proud of his granddaughter-in-law-to-be as he was himself.

"I think it's time Rebecca had a horse of her own again."

Ben gave him a nod and they both walked toward her. She was making a fuss over the adoring horse she had just made look like a quiet donkey, when in fact she was the only one to connect with her at all.

A patter of hooves and a squeal of delight made them all turn. Ben laughed as he watched his daughter come running, as fast as her little legs would carry her, her placid pony in tow. Lexie was holding the end of the lead rope and the pony trotted beside her.

"I thought I told you to wait for us?" Ben said, trying to sound angry and failing. He'd been the same as a kid and he wasn't going to deny Lexie the fun of playing with her pony. That's why he had spent so much getting a kind old horse to teach Lexie the ropes, so he didn't have to worry every time his daughter was out in the field. They were a cute pair, and the pony had been well worth the money.

"You said not to *ride* him on my own," called a breathless Lexie. "See, Mommy? I'm just playing with him, not riding him."

Ben looked at Rebecca and saw her try to hide a smile behind her hand. She had them there; they *had* only said no riding.

"What do you say, *Mommy*?" asked Ben.

Rebecca put one hand on her hip, then burst into laughter as Lexie and the podgy pony ran past.

"Just stay close," Ben called after their adventurous daughter. "And remember she's a horse, not a dog. You need to be careful."

Ben leaned on the rails and watched as Gus approached Rebecca and Missy. He committed to memory the way his grandfather's weathered hand moved in slow circles over the horse's muzzle, then up her neck. The filly certainly responded to Rebecca, but she was partial to Gus, too.

"You did good out there," he heard his grand-dad say.

Rebecca looked up from grooming. "Thanks." She gave the filly a final swoop with the brush then untied her lead rope, ready to walk her back out.

"She'd make a great polo pony if we had any-one decent to ride her, you know," said Gus.

"I know," agreed Rebecca.

Gus pushed his hat up higher to look her in the eye as Ben watched on.

"You never should have lost your horse in that accident, Rebecca." He waited till she looked up before continuing. "You're a great rider and you always will be, which is why I want you to have her."

"No! Gus, she's worth too much and I don't even know if I'd make it through a whole chuk-ker now..."

"I've made my mind up. Don't deny an old man a gift."

"Ben, did you hear that?" Rebecca called out. "Tell him I can't take her."

Ben just grinned and shrugged. “Sorry, but I’m not taking your side on this one.”

“Rebecca, she’s yours. Make me proud. Just promise me that you’ll have fun, and look after that grandson of mine when I’m gone. Okay?”

Ben wiped away a tear as he watched Rebecca walk the horse out into the yard and give Gus an impromptu kiss on the cheek, her arm slung around his shoulders.

“You’re the best granddad in the world, you know that?”

“No, love, you’re the best granddaughter, and I’ve waited a long time to have you. So if I want to spoil you, then so be it.”

Ben jogged the distance to catch up with them, arms looping around Rebecca’s waist once she’d let the horse go.

“We *are* going to have fun, you know that, right?” He kissed her neck, holding her tight. “I love you.”

She turned in his arms, eyes shining with tears. “I love you, too.”

EPILOGUE

BEN SMILED OVER at Rebecca's parents before giving his grandfather a nudge. Gus was standing next to him, dapper in a dark suit and soft pink tie, matching his grandson. He hadn't expected Gus to be on his feet for the ceremony, but the old man was tough as nails and had managed to surprise them all.

A noise from behind stole his attention and Ben laughed when he saw the commotion. Rebecca's brother was trying to coax Lexie down from her pony and wasn't having much luck. From the day he'd given his daughter the friendly little gray gelding, Lexie had hardly given the poor horse a second to relax. It had been love at first sight; his daughter had fallen for the pony as fast as Ben had fallen for his little girl.

There was a whisper through the crowd as the

string quartet started to play, and the soft lull of music made Ben stare at the house, at the door where Rebecca was going to enter from. He held his breath and closed his eyes for a second. When he opened them she was walking toward him. Not on her father's arm, not flanked by a gaggle of bridesmaids, just Rebecca walking toward him, a smile on her face that mirrored his own.

For the first time in his life Ben almost cried in public, but he checked his emotion, swallowed hard and just focused on Bec. Her eyes were shining as she held out her hands to him once she reached him, and he clasped them as tightly as he could before pulling her in for a kiss, just a gentle touch of his mouth to hers to tell her how much he loved her.

Rebecca pressed into him and sighed into his mouth.

"We're meant to wait until after we're married," she whispered, throwing her head back to laugh as he kept her encircled in his arms.

Not the guests behind them, the celebrant clearing her throat, even Lexie standing with her pony and a huge smile, could distract Ben. He had the woman he loved in his arms, and he didn't ever want to let go.

Rebecca squeezed her husband's hand and shook her head as she watched Lexie. She'd refused to come in for the party, preferring instead to race around with her pony, and neither she nor Ben had any intention of forcing her to come in. She was sitting under the shade of the big blue gum tree, sharing food from her paper plate with her four-legged best friend, and there was nothing she'd rather see her little girl doing.

"I love you, baby," Ben murmured in her ear.

Rebecca turned to smile at him and press a kiss to his lips.

The small group of guests were all looking up as metal sounded out on glass. There were no planned speeches but…Rebecca smiled. Gus was standing with his wineglass in hand, clearing his throat. If anyone was going to speak, she was pleased it was him.

"I don't want to talk all night or anything like

that, but someone needs to say a few words about our lovebirds over there," said Gus.

There was a murmur of laughter until his still-strong, deep voice rang out again.

"You probably all know that I haven't got much longer, but what you might not know is just how much I love these two."

He gestured at Rebecca and Ben and she dabbed at the corners of her eyes with her napkin, trying hard not to let any tears spill. To even think about Gus not being around was heartbreaking, especially when she'd gone so many years without seeing him.

"I always knew these two would find a way to be together. As kids, they were inseparable, as young adults, it was obvious to anyone but them that they were in love, and as full-grown adults they were even more stubborn! All I ever heard was nonsense about how they were just friends."

Ben squeezed Rebecca's hand and she laughed. There was no denying how stupid they'd been.

"What I want to say, though, is that these two deserve to be happy, and I know they'll be together for as long as they're living. Which is why I want to present them with the deed to McFarlane Stables."

Rebecca gasped and Ben dropped his glass with a thump to the table. *He what?*

"Before you two protest," continued Gus, waving them away, "I want you to know that I've thought long and hard about this, and the paperwork's already done." He paused, his eyes meeting first hers then Ben's, his smile wide. "So please join with me in raising your glasses in toast to the new Mr. and Mrs. McFarlane, custodians of McFarlane Stables."

Rebecca leaned into Ben and he dropped a kiss to her head. If life couldn't get any more perfect, it just had.

* * * * *